Becky has style, all right. It [is obnoxious.]

is obnoxious.

I lunged into a forward somersault. If you put your hands underneath the beam to hold on, the judges deduct points, so I was being careful to keep my hands on the side, when I heard a voice say, "I've seen more style in a hamburger roll. I heard Patrick telling you that you need style. Maybe I can help. What's your specialty?"

I shrugged. "Patrick says that I'm a good all-around gymnast," I said.

Becky sneered at me. "Oh, one of *those* . . ." she said, laughing.

"What's wrong with being an all-around gymnast?"

"Nothing," said Becky. "It's just that 'all-around' usually means you aren't really good at anything."

I would have killed her, if I didn't have a sneaking suspicion she might be right.

**Other Apple Paperbacks
you will enjoy:**

THE GYMNASTS

#2 FIRST MEET

Elizabeth Levy

AN
APPLE
PAPERBACK

SCHOLASTIC INC.
New York Toronto London Auckland Sydney

To Jean,
who got me into this . . .
and I love it.

ISBN 0-590-41563-8

12 11 10 9 8 7 6 5 4 3 2 1   8 9/8 0 1 2 3/9

Printed in the U.S.A.   11

First Scholastic printing, September 1988

Show Me Who You Are

"Breathe, Cindi!" Patrick commanded. I grunted.

"I want to hear you breathing," Patrick said.

"I'm breathing as hard as I can," I gasped as I completed my twentieth sit-up with Patrick holding my ankles.

Patrick smiled at me. "That's better," he said.

Patrick is my head coach in gymnastics, and normally I love him. I don't mean "love" like have a crush. I just think he's terrific. He's fair, and he's funny. He works us hard, but he never tears us down if we can't do a move. However, I did think maybe he'd gone a little too far in the stomach-crunching direction. Patrick gives each of us an individualized warm-up. Today I was the lucky one who got to concentrate on my stomach muscles.

Patrick's club has an official name, the Evergreen Gymnastics Academy. In reality, the "Academy" is just a cement warehouse on a dusty road about a half mile from the Evergreen Mall outside of Denver. There aren't even any evergreens around, just a bunch of cottonwood trees. There's nothing academic about the way Patrick teaches us. He believes in doing, not talking about it.

Four of us started with Patrick at the same time, and together, he calls us his Pinecones. While I was doing my stomach crunches, Patrick was making Lauren and Darlene do push-ups to work on their upper body strength. Jodi was working on her splits.

Lauren Baca is my oldest friend. She says she's come back to gymnastics just because of me. But she loves it.

Darlene Broderick just turned thirteen. She's two years older than Lauren and me, and she's beautiful. She's always changing her hairstyle. Some days it's loose, and then the next day it will be braided. She has an incredible collection of leotards. Sometimes I think she's got one for every day of the month. Now, me, I like to wear shorts and T-shirts. One thing I like about Patrick's gym is that we have no dress code.

2

Darlene is the daughter of Big Beef Broderick who plays with the Denver Broncos. I've got four older brothers, and since they found out that Big Beef was Darlene's father they've fallen over themselves offering to take me to gymnastics classes and begging me to invite Darlene over.

Jodi Sutton is the fourth Pinecone. She's blonde like me, and she acts like she's tough. Yet she's never exactly what you'd expect. You wouldn't expect a tough blonde kid to wear her hair in a neat braid with ribbons in it, like Jodi does.

Jodi has a lot of upper body strength. She's just not very flexible. Most girls are just the opposite. Trust Jodi not to be like most kids.

Jodi is hard to figure. Her mom was a great gymnast in her day. She coaches the little kids at Patrick's gym. Jodi's sister is on the team at the Air Force Academy in Colorado Springs, but sometimes I think Jodi doesn't take gymnastics very seriously. She can be great one day, and then the next she can't even do the simplest moves.

"All right, " said Patrick, after we had done our warm-ups. "I want to work on three things today: concentration, style, and attitude."

"Oh, no," I groaned. "I hate it when teachers say 'I don't like your attitude.' "

"Right," said Lauren. "What's wrong with my

attitude? I'm here, aren't I? What more do you want?"

"That's exactly it," said Patrick. "I want more. Sometime in the future you girls will be in a competition."

"I don't think we're ready for competition," said Darlene.

"No, not yet," admitted Patrick. "But I want you girls to start thinking like competitors. I've got a lot of confidence in your technique. Now I want to work on attitude."

"All right," said Jodi. "I'll give you more attitude." Jodi stood up and put her nose in the air and balanced on one foot.

"Actually, Jodi, you've got the attitude, but you don't have the concentration. Cindi's got the concentration, but not the attitude."

Jodi and I looked at each other.

"What about me?" asked Darlene.

"You need a little more of both," said Patrick. "I want your routines to be as colorful as your outfits."

Lauren giggled loudly.

Darlene looked a little bit hurt.

"I want you all to try something as we work on the beam today," said Patrick. "Think of yourself as living in a bubble of concentration. You should think of this bubble as surrounding you whenever you are about to do an event. I want you to get in the habit of taking the bubble with you. Each of you has to have your own private bubble."

"Do we get to take it in the bath with us?" I asked. "I love bubble baths."

"I'm not kidding," said Patrick. I looked down. Normally Patrick doesn't mind when we crack jokes.

"Sorry," I muttered.

"Don't worry about it," said Patrick quickly. "Now, I want to talk about style and attitude. Jodi, get up on the beam."

Jodi did a stag mount. It's one of the simpler ways to get on the beam. She threw her chest out and lifted her chin, and she actually looked like a stag leaping onto the beam.

"Do you see?" asked Patrick. "Jodi's got an attitude on the beam. She's made each move her own. Jodi, do a dip walk."

Jodi made a dippy face, and she wagged her head from side to side as she walked along the beam, bending her knees so that her foot dipped below the top of the beam.

"That's a little more attitude than I had in mind," said Patrick. "Get serious."

"Yes, sir," said Jodi.

Jodi curtsied to us, showing off.

"Now do your cat leap," said Patrick. Jodi brought her hands high over her head at the height of her leap, and she really looked like a cat.

"Good," said Patrick. "Come down a minute."

Jodi jumped down, pointing her toes, her hands held high in a beautiful line.

"Do you see what I mean?" asked Patrick. "Jodi's got style. I admit that sometimes she's got too much of an attitude. But she's got her own individual style, and that's what I want each of you to develop. That's what will count with the judges. They'll be looking for something to remember you by. That was good, Jodi. Cindi, let me see you up there."

I pulled the vaulting board over so I could practice my best mount on the beam, a straddle vault to a Japanese split. I jump from the board with my legs wide, and then I go immediately into a split on the beam. I'm lucky because I'm very flexible. I've always been able to do a perfect split, and on the beam a split looks very impressive.

It's the kind of move I love to do in front of my brothers because it makes them go "ouch!"

I did it perfectly.

But Patrick stopped me.

"That's not what I want," he said.

"What did I do wrong?" I asked.

"That's not the point. You *did* it right. It's just that I want to see your style. I want to see what makes that move say Cindi."

"What makes that move Cindi is that she looks like she's splitting in two," said Lauren, always my defender.

I nodded and grinned.

Patrick shook his head. "No, no . . . the split is just something that Cindi was born with. She was born flexible. But I want to see the person Cindi is now. Don't you see the difference?"

I shook my head. I didn't get his point. "I got the move right, didn't I?" I asked.

"Yes, yes . . ." said Patrick quickly. "But attitude . . . I want you to have your own attitude, Cindi. Go work on the low beam and try to come up with something that will show me what you are, and show the judges who you are."

"I'm Cindi," I said. "I never had to worry about who I was before. Who am I? It sounds like a dumb TV show. I'm me."

Patrick didn't laugh. "The judges won't know you, Cindi. They'll see a good, competent gymnast. In fact, you're probably the best all-around gymnast I've got. You're good at all the events. But I want them to see something special. I want them to remember you. Now, get to work. Go over to the low beam, and just work by yourself for a while. See what you can come up with."

I shouldn't have spoken so fast about the academy not being like school. Now I had an assignment.

The low beam has fuzzy, worn yellow carpeting on it. It's only about a foot off the ground, and we all like working on it. It's great to practice somersaults on, because when you fall, you don't have far to go, and the carpeting kind of grabs you and makes you feel secure.

I was just sort of hopping back and forth on the low beam, pointing my toes with each skip. Maybe I had a "bunny" style.

I lunged into a forward somersault. If you put your hands underneath the beam to hold on, the judges deduct points, so I was being careful to keep my hands on the side, when I heard a voice say, "I've seen more style in a hamburger roll."

I fell off the beam onto the mat. I should have known. It was Becky Dyson. She's probably the best gymnast we've got. She'd be the first to tell you she's the best. Becky has style, all right. It's just that her style is obnoxious.

"What do you want?" I asked.

"I want to work on the low beam," said Becky. "I heard Patrick telling you that you need style. Maybe I can help."

"I don't think so," I said. "Patrick said that I should work on finding my own style myself."

"Good luck," said Becky. She did a backbend on the mat next to me, lifting first one foot, then the other to the ceiling. She had incredible flexibility in her shoulders — that's why her walkovers always looked so good. Maybe some people are just born with style.

Becky flipped over. She caught me watching her. "What's your problem?" she asked.

"Actually, I was just thinking how good you are."

Becky shrugged. "That's just one piece of my floor routine. Patrick tells me I'm excellent on floor and the uneven bars."

I shrugged. "Patrick says that I'm a good all-around gymnast," I said.

Becky sneered at me. "Oh, one of those . . ." she said, laughing.

"What's wrong with being an all-around gymnast?"

"Nothing," said Becky, going over to the uneven bars. Becky even walked around the gym in style. She walked with her chest high, and her feet pointed out, like a dancer. She looked back at me, almost pityingly. "It's just that 'all-around' usually means you aren't really good at anything," she said over her shoulder.

I would have killed her, if I didn't have a sneaking suspicion that she might be right.

Gymnasts in Diapers

"Style," I complained to my mother. "I've got no style. Patrick says that I need more style." Mom looked at me.

"You have your own style, Baby," she said.

I glared at her. "That's just the kind of thing a mother would say. And I told you. I don't want to be called 'Baby' anymore."

"You should have named her Cleopatra," said my brother Jared. "Then we could have named the dog Cindi. Cindi's more of a dog's name anyhow." He snorted. Jared's got this disgusting snort that my friends never hear.

My brother Jared and I were cooking dinner. Cleopatra, our dog, was under my feet, hoping I'd drop some food her way. She's a mutt that we got at the ASPCA when she was full-grown. We don't know exactly how old she is. She's very sweet; she just hates to be left alone. Luckily in our house no one is ever left alone for long. Like right now, even though it was Jared's turn to cook and mine to help, everyone else was hanging out in the kitchen.

Tim is sixteen, and Jared is thirteen. My two older brothers are away at college. Once a week Jared or Tim is in charge of dinner. I'm assigned the job of helper. I never have to make the whole meal, or decide what everyone will eat. I won't have to do that until I'm a teenager. I have to do a lot of the dirty work, but I don't mind. At least I don't get blamed for some of the disasters my brothers have come up with.

Tonight I was helping Jared make meat loaf. He had found a recipe for Meat Loaf Surprise. The surprise is disgusting: It's a hard-boiled egg in the middle. I told him it sounded yucky, but he said to trust him.

Jared likes to think that two years make all the difference in the world. He's not half as nice to me as my other brothers. We fight all the time. But he's not all bad. He's a great cartoonist. Every year for my birthday he makes a caricature of me that I frame and hang in my bedroom.

"Actually," said Mom (she starts lots of sentences with "actually"), "Jared, you were the one who started calling her Cindi. You couldn't pronounce Cynthia."

"He always had a lisp," I said.

"CYNTHHHia," sang Jared.

Cynthia is my real name. It's a mouthful. I've never felt like a Cynthia.

Mom tried to ignore both of us. "I always loved the name Cindi. Cinderella was my favorite fairy tale."

"It's okay, Ma," I said. "I wouldn't have wanted to be named anything else." Mom usually takes my side. She worries that my brothers tease me too much. Sometimes I think that just makes them tease me more.

"Besides," I said. "I don't think changing my name will give me style."

"I think your coach is wrong," said Jared. "You have a definite style."

"I do?" I asked eagerly. Maybe my brother was onto something. "What's my style?"

"We-l-l-l," said Jared, dragging out the word. "It's unique. It's a baby style. You can start a new line of leotards. Gymnasts in diapers. It'll be cute."

Jared smirked at me.

"You are a rare treat," I said.

"At least I've got style," he said. Unfortunately Jared was right. He does have style. He's tall and skinny. My other brothers are stockier. Jared plays football on his junior high team. Every time we watch him play, I think he's going to be snapped in half. He looks so delicate. But he's strong.

He wears my dad's old suit jackets with the sleeves rolled up and ratty T-shirts, but he looks good. Lots of my friends think he's really gorgeous. I tell them he's got pimples on his back.

Mom's about the most stylish person I know. She used to be an airline stewardess, and Dad is a pilot. He was out of town tonight.

I have thick hair like my mom's, but I've got my dad's curls, and my hair never stays put. I try to keep it back with rubber bands, but the rubber bands are always breaking. At Christmas, Mom stuffed my stocking with beautiful, glittery ponytail holders. They're not me. They stick out in the back of my hair and make me look weird.

"I wouldn't worry about style," said Mom. "Style is something you'll get when you're older."

"Patrick says that I have to develop my own style *now*," I said. "He doesn't think I have any."

"Did he say that?" Mom asked.

"Not exactly," I admitted. "But I know that's what he thinks. He says that I'm good and all. But I have to do something to make the judges remember me. Jodi has style. Darlene has style. Even Lauren has style."

The phone rang. Jared picked it up. "Baby, it's for you."

"I'm not 'Baby,' " I said.

Jared actually looked apologetic. "I'm sorry," he said. "I forgot. It's Darlene."

I picked up the phone. "What're you doing?" Darlene asked.

"I'm in the middle of helping Jared make meat loaf."

"Well, that's something," said Darlene. "I can't make meat loaf."

"Maybe I should bring some in for Patrick tomorrow to impress him," I said.

"Patrick's impressed with you," said Darlene. "You're the best all-around gymnast in our group."

"All-around just means that you're not good at anything," I said.

"Where did you hear that?" Darlene asked suspiciously. "Did one of your brothers tell you that?"

I laughed. Darlene sounded so serious. Darlene has two younger sisters, and I'm always surprised how seriously she thinks I take my brothers' teasing. I know my brothers can be nasty sometimes, but they're not downright mean.

"No, it was someone who knows more about

gymnastics than all of my brothers put together," I said.

"Becky?" guessed Darlene. "How can you take
anything she says seriously? Remember the
mind games she played on Lauren when we were
doing our first exhibition?"

"I remember." I giggled just thinking about the
handprint Lauren left on Becky's leotard.

"Still, Becky's a good gymnast; you've got to
give her that," I said.

"I don't have to give her anything," said
Darlene.

"Cindi!" yelled Jared. "Am I supposed to do all
the work myself?"

"I've got to go," I said to Darlene.

"Anyhow, I just called to invite you to a party.
Mom says that I shouldn't keep all the different
parts of my life separate, so I'm inviting my gymnastics friends *and* my friends from school."

"Uhh . . . do you think that's a good idea?" I
asked. Darlene goes to St. Agnes, which is the
ritziest private school in our area. The only other
kid at Patrick's who goes to St. Agnes is Becky.
The rest of us go to public school. Besides, Darlene was older than me. I didn't think I'd have
much to say to her friends. "Lauren, Jodi, and
I will be the youngest kids there."

Darlene practically snorted at me. Maybe that's

15

the difference between being eleven and thirteen. "Don't worry about it," she said. "It's three weeks from Saturday night. It'll be fun."

"Thanks for inviting me," I said.

Darlene paused. She sounded uncertain. I wondered if maybe she had hoped I couldn't come. Maybe she had second thoughts about inviting fifth-graders from public school.

"Uh . . . I've got a confession, though," she said.

Uh-oh, I thought to myself. "What's that? You invited Becky?"

"How did you know?" Darlene exclaimed.

"I was kidding," I said. "You didn't really invite her, did you?"

"Mom said that I had to," said Darlene. "Becky's parents are friends of ours, and Mom says since we go to the same school *and* take gymnastics, it would be really mean not to invite her. Besides, Becky just invited me to her party last month."

"She didn't invite Lauren or Jodi or me," I said.

"Forget about Becky. There'll be lots of really nice kids here. It'll be great," said Darlene. "We can dance. We'll show some of my school friends that gymnasts are great dancers."

"Right. . . ." I didn't even have the heart to tell her that I had never danced with a boy who wasn't one of my brothers. I didn't even want to ask her if there would be boys there. Of course there would be boys, and I'd be the baby.

"I've got to go," said Darlene. "I've got to call Lauren and Jodi."

"Okay," I said. "I'll see you tomorrow."

I hung up the phone.

"Okay," said Jared. "Everybody but Cindi out of the kitchen. It's time for us to put in the surprise."

Jared shooed Mom and Tim out of the kitchen. I put the hard-boiled egg on top of the raw meat loaf.

"It goes inside," Jared insisted. "It's supposed to be hidden."

"I think it looks better this way," I said.

"Well, I'm in charge," said Jared. "I'm the one who'll get the blame if there's a rotten egg on top."

He squished the egg into the middle of the meat loaf where it belonged. "What did Darlene want?"

"She's having a party," I mumbled.

"That's terrific," said Jared. "Can I go? I'd like to tell my friends that I went to a party at Beef Broderick's house."

"I don't get invited to *your* friends' parties, so why should you go to mine?"

"Because Darlene's my age."

"Big deal. You're thir*teen*. A teenager, as you're always telling me, and I'm just a kid."

"Are these official United States Gymnastics Federation categories?" asked Jared.

"Yes. . . ." I finished shaping the meat loaf. Maybe I was overreacting. "I'm sorry I snapped your head off, Jared."

"Does that mean I can go?" Jared asked.

I shook my head. "You weren't invited."

"The party should be fun," said Jared.

"They'll all probably be snobs. The one other girl that I know at St. Agnes is a snob. I'll be one of the youngest ones there, and I'll be with a bunch of snobs."

"I bet you'll have a great time," said Jared.

That was easy for him to say. He loved parties. And he had a closetful of clothes that looked great on him.

Now I had two problems. I was supposed to find a stupid style in gymnastics, and I had to figure out what to wear to what would really be my first boy-girl party.

Maybe I could solve them both. Maybe a gymnast in diapers was exactly my style.

Fly Like an Eagle

The next day I watched Becky on the uneven bars. She was working on her "Eagle." It's a hard move. But it's beautiful to watch, because it looks dangerous. She was flying around the bars with no hands. It's the kind of move that impresses the judges. I had been practicing the Eagle, and I knew Patrick thought I was ready to do it, but believe me I was in no hurry to try what Becky was doing.

Patrick was spotting her. But she really didn't need him. If you don't do gymnastics, trust me, what she was doing was scary. I might not like Becky, but she sure is a pleasure to watch on the bars.

I don't think I'm an all-around gymnast, no

matter what Patrick says, and I *know* I'm not really good at the bars. An all-around gymnast is *supposed* to mean that you're equally good at all events. I'm competent on the bars because I've been taking gymnastics for so many years, but I've never felt that comfortable on them.

When I watch someone like Becky, I always think that the next time, I'll be really, really good, and then when I'm up there, I'm just in a hurry to get it over with. But this is my secret. No one knows I feel like that.

Jodi let out a sigh. "Man, she looks good."

"She's got even more good-looking leotards than I do," said Darlene. Becky was wearing a leotard that was light purple on top and then shaded to a deep purple at the bottom. It was beautiful.

"I wasn't talking about her clothes," said Jodi.

"I know," said Darlene. "She just looks so together."

I looked down at my outfit. I was wearing shorts and my special gymnastics "excuse" T-shirt. Mom bought it for me. It lists all the excuses you'll ever need in gymnastics. "I'm afraid of heights. The beam was slippery. I ripped on bars. . . ." I hate ripping on the bars. Sometimes you just take part of the skin right off your palms or you rip open an old blister. That's why you always hear gymnasts say, "I got a rip."

"Okay, Jodi, you're next," said Patrick.

"Can I try the Eagle?" asked Jodi. "It looks like fun."

"That girl is twisted," Lauren whispered to me. Darlene giggled.

"Jodi," said Patrick. "You'll try anything. You aren't nearly ready for the Eagle. Cindi is. In fact, Cindi's been doing the preparation for the Eagle for weeks now."

Lauren poked me in the ribs. "You ready to try that?" she whispered.

I shook my head. "No way," I whispered back.

"What are you wearing to Darlene's party?" Lauren whispered to me. "I told my mom I need a new outfit. I'm excited. A party at the Brodericks! We're moving up in the world. Life-styles of the Rich and Famous."

I made a face. "Yeah, they'll do a separate piece on me. Life-styles of the No Styles. . . ."

"Cindi and Lauren," said Patrick as Jodi chalked up. "If you've got so much energy to talk, go do some conditioning. Let me see ten perfect push-ups, and then twenty perfect stomach crunches."

"We were just whispering about style," I said. "You told me to work on my style. I'm working."

"Let me see you do your stomach crunches with style," said Patrick, laughing at me. "You, too, Darlene. Becky, you can do some conditioning, too."

"I'll lead them," said Becky.

"Good," said Patrick.

I groaned and the four of us went over to the mat. I don't really hate conditioning as much as I pretend to. I actually like the fact that I've gotten stronger and quicker since I've been working with Patrick.

I was counting out my sixth push-up when a stranger walked by and stopped to watch me. He was an older man, and he had on a silver windbreaker with black letters spelling out "ATOMIC AMAZONS." He had curly gray hair.

Jodi was in the middle of her routine, and the stranger walked quickly around the mats and over to the bars to watch her. That's a no-no. Parents and other adults are always warned to keep to the parents' lounge when we're working out. But instead of yelling at the guy, Patrick shook his hand while trying to keep his eye on Jodi so that he could spot her.

"I wonder who that guy is?" I asked.

"That's Darrell Miller," said Becky.

"Thanks, but who's Darrell Miller?"

"Miller is the coach of the Atomic Amazons," said Becky in a tone of voice that implied everyone should know who he is. "He's been winning matches for the past three years. We've never beaten him."

"I looked at his gym," said Darlene. "He runs it like a military school. You have to wear uniform leotards every day. Cindi's T-shirt would be *verboten*."

"Is he the guy Patrick used to work for?" I asked.

Becky nodded. "Yeah. And I heard that he didn't think that Patrick was ready yet for his own school. He thought Patrick was too laid-back."

"Well, that guy doesn't look laid-back," I said.

The man studied Jodi's moves. Jodi really flies on the bars. At one point, she would have slipped off if Patrick hadn't caught her.

Jodi once hurt herself on the bars, but she's not afraid. She doesn't seem to be afraid of anything. Jodi screwed up her dismount. She made a face.

"Concentrate, Jodi," said Patrick. "Courage is fine but without concentration, you'll just get hurt."

Jodi nodded, sweat spots dotting her leotard.

"Cindi, you're next," Patrick yelled to me.

I jumped up and trotted over to the uneven bars. I wanted to impress Patrick's old boss.

"Is this your intermediate team?" the man asked. He didn't even smile at me.

"Yes," said Patrick. "Cindi, this is Darrell Miller. He's another gymnastics coach. Do you mind if he watches you work out?"

I shook my head no. I tried to think about Patrick's bubble of concentration.

"So," said Coach Miller. "Do you have any meets set up for these girls?"

"They're not ready to compete. These are girls who just started working with me, although they had some training before," said Patrick.

"What level are they on?" the man asked.

"Most of them are intermediate, Level IV Class B or C, and I've got another girl who's a very good Class IVA," said Patrick. He put his arm around my shoulder. "I think Cindi here is ready for Class III. In fact, Cindi has been working on the Eagle. We're about to put some of it together."

I raised my eyebrows at Patrick. "We are?"

"You're ready," he said.

I didn't want to contradict him in front of his old boss, but I wasn't at all sure I was ready.

"I'll go chalk up," I said. I always like to chalk up. It's a good excuse not to start right away. We use white chalk dust on our hands to keep from slipping off the bars.

"You don't have to," said Patrick, stopping me.

"We'll start with the 'pop' from the lower bar. Your hands will be free."

"Great," I mumbled.

Patrick lifted me onto the low bar, and he held my legs. "Let go with your hands and just hang there." I hung over the bar.

"Now, you're going to swing your legs, driving against the bar for the bounce," said Patrick. "Don't worry. I've got you."

Patrick did have a firm hold of me, and I knew I wasn't going to fall.

"When I say 'pop,' " said Patrick, "I want you to shoot up your arms and arch your body. Feel like an eagle. Think flying images. It's not called an Eagle for nothing."

I tried the swing. When Patrick said "pop" I shot my arms out. I didn't come anywhere near the high bar, but Patrick was strong enough to lift me the extra three inches, and I was able to grab hold.

"Good," said Patrick. "Let's try it again."

"I'd let her try it herself this time," said Coach Miller. "You don't want her to get dependent on your strength."

"She's just learning it," said Patrick. "Cindi's a very strong girl. But I want her to feel secure."

Hanging over the low bar, upside down, I nodded my head. Believe me, I did *not* want to

25

try that move without Patrick holding on to me.

"You know I don't believe in spotting girls," said Coach Miller. "I realize the non-spotting approach is harder to teach, but — "

Patrick cut him off. "This is not the time or the place for us to have that argument again. I believe in spotting until a girl's ready to do it on her own. We've agreed to disagree. This is *my* gym." Patrick sounded angry.

"Okay, Cindi, let's try it again." Patrick had a firm hold of my hips and legs. I would never have had the courage to shoot my arms out if he hadn't been holding me.

We tried it about six times, and each time Patrick had to lift me to find the high bar, but I did like the "pop." It was fun to shoot my arms out like a bird.

Finally Patrick lowered me to the mats. "Catch your breath," he said. "Then we'll try it once putting the whole move together. I'll talk you through it."

I took a deep breath. We had been working hard.

Coach Miller was frowning at me. I had the feeling that *he* didn't think I had worked hard.

"Patrick," he said. "I've got a problem. My intermediate and lower level girls have been getting ready for a big meet and suddenly the other club got cold feet. I've already booked the judges. It's in three weeks. We'd just do optionals, no compulsories. How about letting your girls have a try at it?"

Coach Miller smiled at me, but it wasn't a nice smile. I wished I had an optional routine that would knock his socks off. In gymnastics, the United States Gymnastics Federation makes up routines for all the events. At some meets, all you do is the compulsory events. But sometimes they'll have meets where each team gets to make up its own routines using elements that we've learned in the compulsories. Optional meets are a lot of fun.

Patrick frowned. "I don't know if they're prepared," he said. "I was going to get up a meet in a couple of months."

"Patrick, you have to let them get used to competition," said Coach Miller in a patronizing tone of voice.

"I'll have to talk it over with them," said Patrick.

"You let your girls decide when you compete?" asked Coach Miller.

"I consult them, yes," said Patrick. Patrick grinned at me. "What do you think, Cindi? You ready for a meet?"

The man with the Atomic Amazons jacket had a superior smile on his face. I wanted to wipe it off.

"Absolutely," I said. "We can be ready in three weeks." Then I looked back up at Patrick. "Can't we?"

"What do you have to lose?" said Coach Miller. Then he coughed as if he were covering up a laugh. "Seriously, Patrick, you'd be doing me a big favor."

"I'll let you know," said Patrick.

"I really need to know today. If you can't do it, I'll ask another club."

Patrick called the other girls over. He explained that the Atomic Amazons were looking for a competition at our level. "It'll just be optionals," said Patrick. "So we can work out our own routines."

"Let's go for it," said Jodi.

"I could use the experience," said Becky.

We took a vote and all of us voted to compete. Coach Miller looked pleased.

Patrick didn't look quite so happy. "Okay, Cindi," he said. "Let's get to work again. I want you to try to put the whole Eagle together while you've still got the feel of it."

I went to chalk up. It's something I always do when I'm nervous. I clapped my hands together to get rid of the loose chalk and took a deep breath before I began my mount.

Patrick smiled at me. "That's good. . . . I want a bubble of concentration around you. This time let's do it with style."

I tried not to giggle. Whenever Patrick says "bubble" I always see myself floating down like the good witch in *The Wizard of Oz*. I grabbed the low bar, and did my mount and kipped to the high bar. Patrick stood underneath me.

"Now you're going to swing out above the bar. Stay extended until the last moment when you hit the low bar. That'll be the force that whips you around. Then you pop up and fly back to the high bar. Okay?"

I nodded. I swung out. I felt Patrick's hands lightly on my legs and knew that he was there. I let go of the high bar, but just at that moment, I got chalk in my eyes. It stung like crazy, and I couldn't see. There I was swinging upside down with no hands. I started to fall. Patrick grabbed me and lowered me to the mats.

I tried to wipe my eyes.

"I got chalk in my eyes," I admitted. It's about the stupidest move you can make on the bars.

Patrick looked at my hands. Chalk was caked between my fingers. It's a mistake that the littlest kids make. They always put too much chalk on their hands, but it wasn't something I was supposed to do.

"Sorry," I mumbled.

"That girl doesn't have a bubble of concentration," said Becky. "She's a dust ball. This competition will be a disaster."

The coach of the Atomic Amazons looked very pleased with himself. I could tell he didn't think we'd be much competition.

I was disgusted with myself, and my eyes really smarted. Patrick patted me on the shoulder. "Go to the bathroom and wash it off," he said. "Don't worry about it." Then he bent down and whispered in my ear. "However, if you get chalk in your eyes during the meet, I'll feed you to the eagles."

He laughed to let me know he was joking. I knew he was joking. The only thing was . . . he didn't know that even before I got chalk in my eyes, I was terrified during that moment that I had to let go. Very scared. I wished I had kept my mouth shut about going for the meet.

A Jerky Style
Won't Win You Points

The next Monday in the locker room, Darlene was putting on her pink leotard with the silver threads. I put on an old pair of shorts and a T-shirt.

I stuck my school clothes in my locker and twirled my combination lock. "So, I guess you're gonna call off your party?" I said to Darlene.

She turned and stared at me. "Huh?"

"Well, it's the same weekend as the meet," I said. "Won't it be too much?"

Darlene put her arm around me. "*You're* too much. Of course I'm not calling off my party. If we win we'll have something to celebrate. If we lose, we can dance to forget."

"Yeah, great," I said.

"I don't know what to wear," said Jodi.

"It's not a formal dance," said Darlene, sounding exasperated. "Wear whatever you feel like."

"Easy for her to say," Jodi whispered to me. "She always looks great."

Just then Becky stuck her head in the locker room. "Patrick is calling a meeting," she said. "and he wants you babies out here, pronto."

"I bet he didn't say 'babies,' " I muttered.

We went out to the gym. Patrick asked us to form a circle around him. "I want to talk about the first meet. The Amazons have asked us to field a five-girl intermediate team. I want to give all the Pinecones a chance, and I'm putting in Becky for her experience. Lauren, you'll be first. Darlene will be second. Jodi, I'm putting you right behind Cindi and Becky."

"What do you mean I go first?" piped up Lauren, sounding a little hysterical. Lauren had just come back to gymnastics after taking off a few years, and she isn't quite as good as the rest of us. But Lauren is strong and she's got guts. "I'm too scared to go first," said Lauren.

"I don't think these infants exactly understand," sneered Becky. "Their role in this meet is to set things up for me."

Patrick scowled at her. "That's not true. We work as a team."

"Right," said Becky. "And the higher these turkeys score, the better it'll be for me. I could even win all-around, couldn't I, Patrick?"

"That's not right. Cindi's the best all-around gymnast," said Darlene. "Isn't she, Patrick?"

"If I'm last," said Becky, "the judges will give me the highest scores. It doesn't matter if Cindi is *sometimes* better on an event than me. The judges won't even notice."

Patrick sighed. "Becky's not completely wrong. The judges expect the best to go last, and they save their highest scores for the last gymnast who performs. The first time I ever competed as a gymnast, all I could think of was 'it's not fair.' I still feel that way. But we have to think of the team. I'm putting Becky last on all the events because she's our best, and I want the judges to get used to looking for her, and giving her the higher scores. I'm sorry, but that's the way it is."

I knew Patrick was telling the truth. A gymnastics meet is weird. There's no equality in gymnastics. I knew that Becky was better than me, and besides I liked being second to last. It was a lot less pressure. Still, I was glad that Darlene thought I was so good.

I must have been daydreaming. Patrick was telling each of us where he wanted us to put in the most work. I was startled when I heard him say my name.

"Cindi, I want you to concentrate on the uneven bars. That's your weakest event, and it's the one event I think we really have a shot at. Now, stretch out, and we'll start work. Becky, when you're ready, you and I will start." He got up to talk to one of the other coaches.

Becky nodded smugly. She poked me in the ribs. "You'd better not foul up, Jockett," she said. "My score will depend on how well you do."

"Don't worry about it," I said. "I'll think bubble."

Becky finished her stretches and went over to Patrick. I stood up to help Lauren stretch out by pushing gently on her lower back while she tried to get her chest to the floor.

"I feel like my bubble is going to burst," said Lauren. "Those Atomic Atoms are going to take one look at me and split in two, laughing."

"Amazons," I corrected.

"I'm really scared," said Jodi.

"You?" I exclaimed. I didn't figure Jodi the type to really worry about anything.

"Yeah, you don't have to worry. You always hit your routines. At least you do if you keep the chalk out of your eyes. With me it's hit or miss." Jodi giggled. I hadn't realized she knew how often she screwed up.

"I have the feeling we're going to be smashed by those Atoms," said Lauren. "Like the atom smasher they have at the Air Force Academy."

"Maybe I can get my sister to come in as a ringer," said Jodi. "There's someone who never fouls up at competition. My sister just loves the crowds. She'd give those Atoms a run for their money."

"It's Amazons," I said. "They're Amazons, not Atoms. Hey, Patrick, is the other team the Amazons or the Atoms?"

"Both," yelled Patrick. "They call themselves the Atomic Amazons." He stood by the side of the uneven bars, observing Becky. I watched, too. Becky did a perfect Eagle without even needing Patrick to spot her once. I knew I couldn't do that.

"That's great," shouted Jodi. "They're the Atomic Amazons, and we're the Evergreens. . . . We're named after a mall. . . ."

"You're named after a tree," Patrick said, not taking his eyes off Becky. He sounded a little annoyed. "Besides, I think calling yourselves something like the Atomic Amazons stinks. How's a girl going to feel if she's *not* an Amazon?"

"With our name, we can call 'Tim-*ber* . . .' when we fall," I said. "It can be our rallying cry." I meant it as a joke, but Patrick didn't laugh.

Becky completed her dismount. Patrick congratulated her.

"I think Evergreen is a great name," said Lauren. "The evergreens take over the forest. Up in the mountains, the aspen trees grow after a forest fire, but eventually the forest gets taken over by the evergreens because they grow taller and stronger. It's a proven fact."

Patrick laughed. "Lauren, you're always coming up with these weird facts. I love it. Anyhow, let's not worry about names right now. Cindi, come up here, my little Pinecone. It time you turned into an Evergreen."

"Maybe I can be an artificial Christmas tree," I said. "You know, all in silver. Then I won't have to grow anymore. I'm worried about getting too tall."

"Just worry about working a little harder on your Eagle," said Patrick.

I looked at him. Was it my imagination? Or was Patrick laughing at the other kids' jokes, but not at mine? It seemed lately that Patrick wanted a lot from me.

"Okay, Cindi," he said. "Let's see you work on the Eagle again," he said.

I groaned. Even with Patrick spotting me, I missed the catch to the high bar more often than I got it.

I started the move and I thought I was doing fine. Patrick stopped me. "Do it again," he said. "You've got to use all your strength to push above the high bar with your arms straight. Come on,

Cindi, you're strong enough to make this look *right*."

"I'm trying," I said.

"Try again," said Patrick. "This time concentrate — "

"Right, I lost my bubble," I said. "It's better than losing my marbles, huh?"

"A little less chatter and a little more taking this seriously," said Patrick.

I nodded, but I was getting angry. I tried it again. Patrick stood underneath to catch me if I missed the high bar. I really hated this move. I couldn't see the high bar; I had to "sense" where it was. I knew I'd fall straight down if Patrick wasn't underneath me.

"Cindi," Patrick grunted from the effort of holding me up. "That's the lousiest I've seen you do it. It's as if you've got no idea where the high bar is. The judges are going to hate it when you look so awkward."

"I don't want to do this move in the meet," I said. "I'm not ready. Can't we cut it?"

"No," said Patrick. "It's a pretty move, and so impressive. You and Becky are the only ones we have who can do it. I want to leave it in. But you're concentrating so hard on just doing it, you don't have any style."

I groaned. "Oh, no, not style again."

Patrick didn't look amused. "Cindi, it has to look as if you and the movement are one. You can't do the Eagle half-heartedly. It's a move that demands your own aggressive style."

"But I'll never do it without you spotting me," I said. "Why are we even bothering?"

"Yes, you will," said Patrick. "You're very close. It's just that you panic and your timing gets off."

I nodded my head.

Patrick looked annoyed with me. "Are you really listening to me, or just nodding?"

I nodded again. We were having this conversation with me holding myself up over the high bar. I could feel the sweat dripping down from my forehead into my eyes. I was having a hard time holding my position.

Patrick smiled at me. "If it was easy, everyone would do it," he said. "Come back down and do it again."

I let myself down from the high bar and stood on the blue mat. I was so angry I couldn't even look up at Patrick.

"Again?" I cried.

"Again," repeated Patrick. "This time, as soon as you get up on the high bar, don't rest."

"I wasn't resting," I complained. "I was listening to you."

"You were resting," said Patrick. "In the bars, it's got to flow. Cindi, you've got to keep several

38

things in your head at once. You've got to concentrate on the move you're doing . . . complete it, but you can't stop . . . everything has to flow. You're jerky on the bars. You complete each move but then you pause a beat. A jerky style won't win you points."

"Thanks," I muttered. "Jerky?"

Patrick nodded. "I'm only being hard on you because I think you can do so much better."

"Do you mean, it's for my own good?" I asked sarcastically. I hate it when my parents tell me to try harder. At this moment I hated Patrick.

But then he smiled at me. I don't think he had a clue how angry he was making me.

"I mean it, Cindi," said Patrick. "I want you to concentrate."

I tried the Eagle again. This time I missed the catch completely, and would have come crashing down if Patrick hadn't caught me. Unfortunately when Patrick tried to break my fall, my leg went into his stomach and he groaned.

"Sorry," I muttered.

Patrick tried to catch his breath. "Are you trying to kill me?" he asked, only half joking.

"No," I said, but I was only half joking, too. I didn't like having to work so hard.

Patrick put his arm around me. "Cindi, look. I know you're mad at me."

I didn't lift my eyes. "I'm not mad," I lied.

Patrick laughed. "You're allowed to get mad at your coach. That's human. But I want you to get it right. Okay, take a break. I want to work with Lauren on her floor exercise. But I want you to think about the move. Think about how to make it your own."

The Eagle Falls

I plunked down on the mat next to the uneven bars and wiped the sweat from my neck with the edge of my T-shirt.

Jodi came and sat beside me. "Having a hard time?" she asked.

I nodded. "I'd like to stuff the Eagle back into a cage. I'll never get it, and Patrick won't let me quit."

"I wish I was good enough to try it," said Jodi, looking up at the bars. "You came close. You'll get it soon."

Becky walked by us. "Why are you Pinecones just lying on the ground?" she asked. "You should be working. We only have a few weeks before the meet. I don't want my teammates to foul up. I saw you try the Eagle, Cindi. You stunk."

"You are *so* supportive," said Jodi. "The kind of teammate every gymnast dreams of having."

"What's that supposed to mean?" asked Becky.

"Why don't you do something instead of tearing Cindi down?" said Jodi. "My sister's always helping her teammates with moves that they can't do."

Becky looked thoughtful. She swung back and forth on the low bar. I didn't think she was really going to help me, but I could tell that Jodi's words had hit home. "I suppose I could give you the benefit of my expertise," Becky said.

Jodi closed her eyes. "Right, that's exactly how my sister offers to help," she said.

"Really?" said Becky.

Jodi laughed. "I was kidding, Becky. My sister doesn't put everyone else down. Well, maybe *me* sometimes, but not her teammates."

"So, what do you want me to do?" Becky asked, exasperated.

"Help Cindi," said Jodi. "After all, you're doing the Eagle without a spot already."

Becky looked over at me. "So what's giving you the problem?" she asked.

"Well, Patrick keeps telling me to do it with style. But it happens so fast, and I'm so scared that I'm not going to even catch the high bar, that I can't think of style."

"MY style just comes naturally," said Becky. "I'll show you." She walked over to the chalk bin and chalked up. "I'll do it slow for the slow," she said.

"Don't the judges take points off for sneering?" I said.

Jodi gave me the thumbs-up sign. "Good one," she whispered.

"Now watch me very closely," said Becky.

"Wait a minute," I said as Becky grabbed the low bar. "Are you sure you should do the Eagle without Patrick?" Patrick was at the other end of the gym working on Lauren's floor routine.

"I don't need a spot," said Becky. "I'm going to be doing it on my own in the meet."

Becky stood in front of the lower bar. I had to admit that for a moment she looked as if she had Patrick's "bubble" of concentration surrounding her. The sneer left her face, and just before her mount, she had a look of total concentration.

Then she swung up, and I could see what Patrick meant by the fact that it all flowed.

She paused on the high bar and looked down at me. "Cindi, pay attention," she ordered.

"I am," I said.

"You'll see when I start my move, I sort of hollow out," she said.

"She's hollow," whispered Jodi.

"Shh," I said, trying to concentrate on Becky. She might be a pain, but the truth was she did this move much better than me. I thought I could learn from her.

She swung onto the low bar and let go, her body just slightly hollowed out so that she could get the most momentum without using her hands.

Then she arched her back, threw her arms over her head like an eagle, reaching for the high bar behind her. But she missed the high bar, and instead of landing on both legs, she had all the weight on her right leg.

"OUCH!" she screamed, and she sank to the floor.

It didn't look like that bad of a fall, but Becky was crying and screaming in pain.

6

Gymnastics Is Much Tougher Than Football

"What happened?" cried Patrick. He raced across the floor in record time. He kneeled down beside Becky. "Tell me where it hurts," he asked softly.

"It's my ankle," Becky sobbed. "My ankle."

"Cindi, get ice," Patrick snapped. I was glad that he had given me something to do. I ran to the refrigerator that sits next to the parents' lounge. The one luxury that Patrick insisted on was an automatic ice machine so that there is always plenty of ice on hand for injuries. I filled a plastic bag with ice and hurried back over to Becky.

Jodi's mother saw me running with the dripping bag of ice. "What's wrong?" she asked.

"Becky fell," I said. Mrs. Sutton ran with me back to the uneven bars. "Is she badly hurt?" she asked Patrick. "How did it happen?"

"She was showing me the Eagle," I said. "She twisted as she fell."

"Why was she doing it without Patrick?" demanded Mrs. Sutton.

Jodi and I looked at each other. We both felt guilty. "I told her maybe she should wait for a spot," I said.

"You were the one who asked for help with your stupid style," snapped Becky. "I was trying to do it slow for Cindi." She held her foot and glared at me.

"None of that matters," said Patrick. "We can sort it out later. Let's just see how you are."

Patrick felt Becky's ankle. Even I could see that it was already swelling up. It was scary to think how quickly an accident like that could happen. She was really in pain. She had no color in her face, and she kept her eyes closed tight as if that would make the pain go away.

"Breathe, Becky," said Patrick. "Come on, honey, take some deep breaths. You're going to be okay."

"It hurts," Becky sobbed. "It hurts more than anything."

"I think we'd better take her for X-rays," said Patrick.

Jodi's mom nodded.

"Patrick . . . it hurts so bad," said Becky.

Patrick kept his hand on her shoulder, trying to comfort her. "I know, and I believe you." He looked up at Jodi's mom. "Becky's got a high pain tolerance. If she's hurting this much, it must be bad. I think it's just a sprain, but it might be broken or a chipped bone. I'll drive her. You give Dr. Vickers a call and tell him I'm on my way."

Becky caught us staring at her. "What are you looking at?" she yelled.

"We just wanted to be sure you were okay," I said.

Becky turned her face away from me. "Is there anything I can do?" I asked Patrick.

"She'll be okay," said Patrick. "Becky, I wish you would have remembered that you shouldn't do that move without a coach watching. Cindi, why don't you take the Pinecones over to the mats and work on your conditioning? I want twenty stomach crunches and twenty push-ups, okay?"

"Why me?" Becky wailed. "Why did it have to happen now? I don't *need* an accident right now."

Patrick nodded his head. "Nobody needs an accident. But we'll see how you are — "

"But what if I can't compete?" Becky wailed. "It *would* have to happen now."

"One step at a time," said Patrick to Becky. "Let's get X-rays and we'll see what happened to you."

Patrick looked up. We all hadn't moved. We were still standing in a circle like statues, staring at Becky.

Mrs. Sutton came back with the plastic splints that Patrick kept in his first aid kit in his office. In the time that I had been working with Patrick, no one had ever needed them.

Patrick was expert at putting on the splints with velcro bindings. Then he helped Becky to her feet and picked her up like she weighed nothing.

He saw us staring at him, but he didn't seem angry. "Cindi . . . go on now, lead the others in some conditioning. Becky's going to be all right. After you finish your conditioning, you girls can go home. I'll see you tomorrow."

"Good luck, Becky!" I shouted.

Becky didn't answer back.

Patrick glanced back at me. "Conditioning," he said.

I led the other Pinecones to the mats. We had work to do. We finished our conditioning in record time. Everyone was talking about Becky's accident.

Gloria, Becky's best friend, asked me how it happened. "She was showing me her Eagle," I admitted.

Gloria glared at me. "And now she's hurt, and you're fine."

"It's not my fault that I didn't hurt myself," I said. Gloria stomped away from me.

Lauren tugged on my arm. "Come on," she said. "Don't mind her. Let's go get changed."

I went into the bathroom. My hands were full of chalk dust from working on the bar. My hands hurt when I washed them. The water stung my palms. My hands often hurt after doing bars, but this time the tiny stinging pain reminded me of Becky. I couldn't stop thinking about her.

Jodi came into the bathroom. She looked pale, too. "Do you think Becky's okay?" she asked.

"Yeah," said Darlene, coming in behind her. "Who ever thought I'd ever worry about Becky, but that fall was scary."

"I've seen worse," said Jodi. "Once Mom was doing the Eagle and she completely missed the bar, and scraped her whole leg open. You could actually see the bone."

"That's gross," said Darlene, looking a little sick.

"Well, I'm just saying that what happened to

Becky isn't that bad. I bet she'll be back and just as obnoxious as ever," said Jodi. "Except I feel a little guilty. I sort of goaded her into helping Cindi."

"How do you think I feel? She practically blamed me," I said.

"She'd blame anyone except herself," said Jodi. "You warned her not to do it without a spot."

"I bet that if Becky does need a cast it'll come in a designer color," said Lauren.

"Uh-huh," said Darlene. "She'll make the doctor give her a different cast for every day."

"Yeah, plaids for Monday, stripes for Tuesday . . ." I said, giggling.

Just then Gloria stalked into the bathroom.

"How can you laugh after what just happened to Becky?" she asked.

"We're not laughing," I said guiltily.

Darlene giggled.

"You are, too," said Gloria. "I heard you laughing in here. You sounded like a bunch of hyenas. I think it's horrid. This could be a tragedy for the Evergreen team. Do you realize that we'll have zilch chances if Becky's out for the meet? She was the only one in your class who had a chance." Gloria was an elite gymnast.

Lauren stared at her. "You're her best friend, and that's what you're worried about?"

Gloria glared at Lauren as if realizing what she had said. "Well, it's what Becky would have wanted me to worry about," she said huffily.

I covered my mouth. I wanted to laugh so much I thought I was going to burst.

Lauren caught my eye, and immediately grabbed her stomach. I knew Lauren. We were going to be in trouble. We get these laughing spells sometimes where we can't stop laughing, even when it's totally inappropriate. Lauren tried not to look at me.

Gloria turned her back and stalked out of the bathroom. Lauren and I both opened our mouths and started to howl.

"What's so funny?" asked Jodi.

I tried to catch my breath. I hiccuped. "Nothing. . . ." Then I caught Lauren's eye and we started laughing again.

"It's just. . . ." I couldn't catch my breath. "Even Becky's best friend is more worried about the competition than about her."

"I bet Becky's already sorry that we didn't get her fall on videotape for her archives," said Darlene.

"We shouldn't be laughing," said Lauren and then proceeded to start laughing again for no reason.

"Maybe we should make Becky a get-well card," I said. "We could do one on my computer. It has

51

a program for drawing birthday cards and get-well cards."

"Does it have a list of sick jokes?" asked Lauren.

"No. You're my walking computer of sick jokes. Don't you know any regular feet jokes we can use?"

"What wears shoes, but no feet?" asked Lauren.

I was stumped.

"The sidewalk," said Lauren triumphantly.

"I don't get it," said Darlene.

"See, the sidewalk will wear out your shoes," said Lauren.

"That's dumb," said Jodi.

"Dumb, but not sick," said Lauren.

"How does she remember so many bad jokes?" Jodi asked.

"She's got a photographic memory," I said. "She can memorize whole pages of books."

"How do you stop her?" asked Darlene.

"You don't," I said. "Once she gets going, she's on automatic pilot."

"I've got another foot joke," said Jodi. "We can use this if we handwrite the card. Why is writing called handwriting?"

We all looked at her blankly.

"Because if people wrote with their feet, we

would have to call it footwriting," mumbled Jodi.

"Enough," I shouted. Jodi was an awful joke-teller. "Why don't you all come to my house, and we'll make the get-well card?"

"I wouldn't mind that," said Darlene. "Will Jared be there?"

I shrugged. "Who cares?"

"I just wondered. He's great at drawing cartoons. Maybe he can help us make a get-well card."

"He doesn't even know Becky," I objected.

"Well, I was just asking," said Darlene. "Besides I was wondering if maybe he wanted to come to my party."

"Why would you want to invite him?" I asked.

"Because some of my friends at St. Agnes want to meet new boys," said Darlene. "Do you think he'll want to come?"

"How would I know?" I asked. Actually I did know. I knew Jared wanted to go to Darlene's party.

As we walked out of the gym, I tugged on Lauren's arm. "Do you think it was my fault that Becky got hurt?" I asked.

Lauren stared at me. "You're out of your gourd," she said.

"Thanks," I said. "That's comforting."

Both Jared and Tim were waiting for us when

we got out. Jared jumped out of the Jeep when he saw us. "Hi," he said. "How are the Old Tumblers?"

"We're gymnasts, Jared," said Lauren. " 'Old Tumblers' makes us sound like some glasses you picked up at a yard sale."

"That Lauren, always joking," said Jared. I was glad to hear his voice cracking.

"Jodi, you know my brothers," I said. "The one driving is Tim. The insane one, here, is Jared."

"Jared, why do they call you crazy?" asked Jodi.

"The same reason they call vampires crazy," I said.

"Why's that?" Jodi asked, always the perfect straight person.

"Because Jared is bats," I said.

"Very funny," said Jared.

"Actually, I thought it was," said Darlene.

"Jared's not crazy. He's just got growing pains," I said. "He's a growing pain."

"It's not Jared's fault that he's tall," said Darlene.

"Thank you, Darlene," said Jared. "My family seems to think my height is a good joke."

"My dad is six feet four."

"Yeah, but he's got muscle. . . . Jared is just long and skinny as a pencil," I said. "But you know the difference between Jared and a pencil?"

"What's that?" asked Darlene.

"There's no point to Jared," I said.

Jared gave me a knuckle sandwich on my head. "Ouch. That really hurts," I said, backing away from him. "You are such a jerk. You should be nice to us, we've had a trauma."

"What trauma?" asked Tim.

"A girl in gymnastics got hurt," I said, as I jumped into the backseat. "Everyone's coming to our house."

"Who got hurt?"

"Becky Dyson. She's sort of a creep," said Lauren.

"That's a nice thing to say about one of your own," said Jared.

"Well, I'm just telling the truth," said Lauren.

"Besides, we're not being mean," I said. "Everyone's coming over to make a get-well card."

"Oh, good," said Tim, sarcastically. "I felt the need to have the gymnastics team doing cartwheels while I'm trying to write a term paper."

"We'll keep out of your way. But I need the computer," I said. "We have work to do, too."

"So, are you guys ready for your first meet?" asked Jared. "Cindi's got it in red letters on our calendar. Right before Darlene's party."

"Hint, hint," I whispered to Lauren.

"Oh," said Darlene. "Jared, I meant to ask you. Would you like to come with Cindi?"

I practically doubled over laughing. There was no way Jared wanted to come *with* me. He wanted to go to Darlene's party, but not with his little sister.

"Uh . . . maybe . . ." stammered Jared. He looked back at me. "You don't mean as Cindi's date?"

Darlene giggled. "No . . . I just meant . . . did you want to come . . . *you* know."

"These *teen*agers are certainly having an intelligent conversation," I said.

"Both of you, lay off," said Tim. Tim hates it when Jared and I start fighting in his car. He says it distracts him.

Tim tried to change the subject. "I'm looking forward to your meet," he said. "Cindi comes to our football games. It's about time we returned the favor."

"Yeah, well, if Becky doesn't recover quickly, it's gonna be one big fiasco," I said. "You might as well stay home."

"What exactly happened?" Jared asked.

We told him all the details of Becky's accident.

"That's nothing," said Tim. "You remember when I separated my shoulder? They taped me up and I was still able to play. She'll probably be okay."

"Gymnastics is much tougher than football," I said. "You should read our safety instructions. They're full of warnings about catastrophic death."

"Can we change the subject?" asked Lauren. "I'm getting carsick."

"Open the windows," said Tim as he sped up.

The Dread Word

Jared actually begged me to let him help us make the card. He thought it sounded like an interesting project.

"No," I said.

My friends stared at me. "But Jared's good," said Lauren. I gave her a dirty look. Didn't my friends think that I could do *anything* myself?

"It was my idea to make her a get-well card," I said. "If you want to have Jared make her one, you can, but it won't be from me."

"Hey I'm sorry. You don't have to snap my head off," said Lauren.

"Look," said Jared. "I was just offering. It doesn't matter to me."

"Then just let us use the computer without you," I said.

The computer is set up on a desk in the guest room, and my brothers and I have a schedule of when we can use it. Naturally I get to use it the least, because I'm the youngest and don't need it as much for my schoolwork.

Jared slammed the door to the guest room. "What's wrong with you?" Darlene asked me.

"Nothing," I said, sitting down at the desk. "I just get sick of people thinking I need help all the time."

I sat down at the computer and drew a series of pictures showing a gymnast swinging from the bars doing the Eagle.

"What do you have there?" Jodi asked.

"I'm trying to make it look like the Eagle," I said.

"It does," said Jodi. She called the others to come look over my shoulder.

"That's really good," said Darlene, sounding surprised.

I corrected the proportions.

Next I had the computer draw in big letters, HOPE YOU'LL BE SWINGING AGAIN.

"It's terrific!" exclaimed Jodi.

"Yeah," said Lauren. "It's almost too good for her. Maybe we should keep it for one of us. We're bound to get hurt one of these days."

I made a face at Lauren. "That's sick."

"I say we send it to Becky. But let's make another copy so we can show Patrick," said Darlene.

"So, what do we sign it?" I asked as the printer clacked it out.

" 'Love, the Pinecones'?" Darlene suggested.

Lauren held her nose. "I'm not sure I can sign 'love' to Becky."

"I sign 'love' when I write thank-you notes to relatives I've never met," said Darlene.

"That's different. It's not a downright lie," Jodi said. "How about just signing our names?"

"That seems cold now that we've gone to all the trouble to make the card," Darlene said.

"Becky is definitely not lovable," said Lauren.

"How about a picture of a heart and a pinecone?" I suggested. "I could have the computer draw it."

I drew a heart and a pinecone on the computer.

"That's adorable," said Darlene.

"It's disgustingly sweet," said Lauren. "Icky. It looks like something on a greeting card."

"It *is* on a greeting card," I pointed out.

I printed it out again, and pulled the paper out of the printer. I studied my computer art. "This is terrific," I said, "if I do say so myself. Does anyone know Becky's address?"

"Why don't you bring it to gymnastics class

tomorrow?" suggested Jodi. "That way we can show it to Patrick. It's too great just to give to Becky."

"I agree," said Darlene. "It's got style." I glanced at her to see if she was teasing me.

"What's wrong?" asked Darlene.

"Nothing," I said.

"Why did you suddenly start looking at me like I was Jason in *Friday the Thirteenth*?" Darlene asked.

"I didn't," I protested.

"You said the 'dread' word," said Lauren.

"What dread word?" asked Darlene.

"The S word," said Lauren.

"So powerful the mere mention of it made Becky break her leg," said Jodi, giggling.

"Cut it out," I said.

"What are they talking about?" Darlene insisted.

I sighed. "They're just teasing me. Remember how Patrick's on my back about developing my own attitude and style? It bothers me. And I don't know what to wear to your party."

"You've got plenty of style," said Darlene.

I raised my eyebrows. "I do?" I remembered Jared's crack about gymnasts in diapers.

"Yeah, it's a casual style. But I like what you wear to classes. You look cute in shorts."

"I can't wear shorts to your party," I said.

"What's your problem?" asked Darlene. "With all those older brothers, just raid their closets. You'll look great."

"I will?" I asked.

"Sure," said Darlene. "Come on." She marched down the hall to Jared's room.

"Jared, open your closet door," insisted Darlene.

"You've got to be kidding," said Jared.

"I am not," said Darlene with her hands on her hips. "I just wish I had an older brother. Let me see what you've got in here. Cindi needs something to wear to my party."

"I do not need anything he's got in there," I said.

"Right, you don't need my help at all," said Jared. "How did your little get-well card come out?"

"It's great," said Lauren. She showed it to Jared.

"A heart and a pinecone," said Jared. "That's so sweet. It looks like something from kindergarten. Why don't you wear that to Darlene's party?"

"Give me back the card," I said. "You'll ruin it with your dirty fingers. Let's get out of here."

"Wait a minute," said Darlene. "I bet Jared's got a lot of things you can wear. Just cool your jets. Jared, please, let me just see what you've got in there."

Jared opened his closet. There were so many clothes stuffed in there that the hangers were five deep on the floor. "I could be buried alive if I go in there," Darlene said. "How did you get so many clothes? That closet is fuller than my dad's, and he loves clothes."

"I get all my brothers' hand-me-downs," said Jared. "I'm the last of the line."

"Some of these will be great on you, Cindi. Go in there, and come out with a sports jacket," said Darlene, my commander. "In fact, come out with a couple. I want one. Jodi, what are you wearing to my party?"

Jodi shrugged. "I haven't thought about it."

"I have a new jumpsuit," said Lauren.

"It'll look great with one of these jackets," said Darlene.

I held my breath and dove into Jared's closet. I came out with my hands full of my brother's clothes, including an old tuxedo jacket that used to belong to my father.

"That is fantastic," said Darlene. She tried the tuxedo jacket on me. It was huge. "That's great," she said.

"It is?" I looked at myself in the mirror. I looked weird. "I hate it."

Darlene rolled the sleeves up, and put up the collar.

"There," she said. "That's the look."

I turned around in the mirror. "I still hate it," I said. "I look ridiculous."

Darlene looked exasperated. She took the jacket off me.

"Can I try it?" Jodi asked.

"Oh, why not?" asked Jared. "Why doesn't everyone just use my clothes?"

Jodi tried the jacket on. She twirled around in the mirror. "I love it. Can I borrow this?" she asked Jared.

Jared looked at Darlene. "Sure," he said. "Take what you want." I knew if Darlene hadn't been there, he would have said no.

"This still doesn't solve Cindi's problem," said Darlene. She held out one of Jared's plaid shirts.

"Try this on," she said.

I tried it on. I looked like a boy out of *Little House on the Prairie.*

"It's not me," I said.

"It's different," said Darlene.

"But I hate it."

"You can't just say you hate everything," said Darlene, sounding annoyed. "I love that on you. It's you."

"It is not," I said, a little louder than I expected.

"Then what *is* you?" Darlene asked.

I glared at her. I was getting awfully sick of people asking me that question.

I threw Jared's shirt on the floor.

"I don't know," I said. "But when I find out, you all will be the first to know."

I stomped back to my room. Darlene, Jodi, and Lauren followed me.

"What was that all about?" asked Darlene. "That jacket *did* look good on you. And that shirt was even better."

"I hated how I looked in them," I said. I looked at myself in the mirror. "I need something different, but it has to be *me*, don't you understand?"

"I understand. I can't let anyone else pick out things for me. You'll find something you like. I always do," said Darlene.

I knew she did. Darlene did have her own style. It showed in everything she did. It was me that was the problem. The "dread" word, Lauren had called it. She had been joking, but the joke no longer seemed funny.

8

This Eagle's a Dodo

The next day Lauren's mom drove us to gymnastics class.

"Did you bring the get-well card?" Lauren asked.

I nodded. We showed it to Lauren's mother who pronounced it "darling." Lauren's mom works for the Board of Education, and she's not the type to say she likes something if she doesn't. I put the card back in the envelope, feeling quite proud of it.

We walked into the gym, and who should be sitting in the big easy chair in the parents' lounge, but Becky herself. She had a cast on the lower part of her leg.

A group of girls including Darlene and Jodi were sitting at her feet, and Patrick was standing over them.

Lauren and I got closer and we saw that everybody on the floor had a piece of paper in front of them.

"Becky, how are you?" I asked, staring at her cast.

"It's a *very* bad sprain," said Becky, sounding a little disappointed that it wasn't a break. "But the doctors put it in a walking cast so that I would keep it immobile. I can't do any gymnastics for a month. You can sign my cast, but first you have to submit a drawing."

Darlene coughed. "Becky wants us to submit drafts of our signatures before she lets anybody sign it."

"So many kids let just anybody sign their casts," said Becky. "It ends up looking like something from kindergarten."

I caught Darlene's eye. She was having trouble not laughing. "I'm sure Princess Diana would act the same way if she had a broken leg," said Darlene.

"That's right," said Becky. Sarcasm was lost on her.

"Why don't you show Becky our card?" suggested Lauren. "Maybe she can paste that on her cast."

"Maybe we can paste it on her nose," whispered Jodi.

"We Pinecones made you a get-well card," I said, handing Becky the card.

She hardly glanced at it. Patrick took it from her. "This is terrific," he said.

I blushed. "I did it on the computer," I said.

"It's wonderful," said Patrick.

"Let me see it again," said Becky.

Patrick handed it to her. She showed it to Gloria and her other friends. "This isn't all that bad," she said.

"I would use the word 'great,' " said Patrick.

I grinned at him.

Becky looked at the card critically, "Stop drawing, everybody!" she commanded. She turned to me. "Put this on my cast." She pointed to the stick figure swinging on the bars.

"Huh?" I said.

"I don't want *any* names on my cast," said Becky. "Everyone who has a broken arm or leg has signatures. It's been done. But if you put this drawing on my cast, everyone will know that I hurt myself doing gymnastics." Becky looked up at Patrick. "Don't you think it'll be neat?"

Patrick smiled at me. "It'll be neat, but I don't know if Cindi can do it . . . or wants to. . . ."

"She owes me," said Becky. "Of course, she'll

do it. I hurt myself demonstrating the Eagle for her."

"Well, I don't know," I said. "I did it on the computer; I'd have to trace it on your cast."

"Great," said Becky, as if it were all settled. She stuck out her leg. I guess I really did owe her something. I sat at her feet and tried to trace the drawing on the cast. I almost wished Jared was there. It was really an interesting problem having to do it on such a lumpy surface. It came out pretty good, if I do say so myself.

Becky looked at it critically. "Can't you make the girl look more like me?" she asked. My back ached from working crouched down on the floor.

"Yeah, put a tiara on it," said Darlene. "After all, you're the queen around here."

"A tiara would be nice," said Becky.

Lauren cracked up.

"What's so funny?" Becky demanded.

Patrick looked at my drawing on Becky's cast. "It's wonderful," he said. "Now, I think we've spent enough time on Becky's cast. Let's go into the gym."

Patrick put his arm around me. "You're a good kid, Cindi," he said. "Now, how about a little gymnastics? With Becky out of the meet, I'm going to put you last up. I'll be counting on you."

"Not on me," I blurted out.

Patrick laughed. He thought I was joking. I wasn't. I felt sick.

We went into the gym, and Becky hobbled next to me. All during my warm-ups, I kept hearing Patrick say, "I'll be counting on you."

We worked on our floor routines first, and I was great. My one-armed cartwheel was perfect. And then I hit the back handspring into a round-off. It wasn't just that I hit all my tumbling runs. I was good in between moves, too. My hands felt right. My arm movements felt right. I was breathing with my moves. I even ended in time with the music. I knew it was one of the best routines I had ever done.

"Good job, Cindi," said Patrick as I stepped off the mat. He shook my hand, making me feel very grown-up.

Maybe it would turn out that Becky's injury was just the spur I needed.

Then we went to the uneven bars. "Okay," said Patrick. "Let's see your routine."

Patrick moved away to the side of the bars. "Where are you going?" I asked.

"It's time for you to try it without me," he said. "You don't need a spot."

"Yes, I do." I said.

"Try it," said Patrick. "And Cindi, put some style into it. Remember how the girl in your drawing looked? She looked like she was flying.

I want to see that flair in you. I want to see Cindi fly."

I concentrated right before my mount. I was sure I could do it just like Patrick said. I would fly like a bird. I grabbed the lower bar and swung myself up, grabbing the high bar. "Fly, fly," I said to myself. I was working as hard as I could. I swung into my Eagle, but when I let go of the high bar, I hit the low bar wrong. I didn't have enough momentum to get around. I was stuck, hanging from my stomach.

I slipped off to the mat. "Sorry, this Eagle turned back into a dodo."

Patrick didn't smile. "Try it again," he said.

"I need a spot," I said. "I can't get around on my own."

"Try it, Cindi," he said.

I sighed and grabbed the low bar again. Once again my mount went fine, but when I tried the first part of the Eagle, I got stuck. I just didn't have enough power to get around the bar.

"We'd better change my routine," I said. "I'll never get that move by the time of the meet."

"That's for me to decide," said Patrick. "You've got the power; you need the will."

"But I was great doing my floor exercise," I said.

"I know," said Patrick. "But the floor and the beam are easy for you. I want you to fight harder on the bars. That's the challenge. Let's make a deal. I'll continue to spot you on that move for the rest of the week. On Monday, I want you to try it yourself."

"I won't be ready," I said.

Patrick didn't look angry. "Just think about it. Darlene, you're next."

Darlene did her routine. Darlene is a hoot on the bars, literally. She makes little shrieks every time she completes a circle.

It cracked Patrick up. "If you do that for the judges at the meet, I'll kill you," he said, still laughing.

Darlene knew he was kidding. She caught her breath and laughed.

Why was he so easy on Darlene and hard on me? That's what I wanted to know.

I didn't have the answer.

I wished that Becky had never hurt herself. I wished that the coach of the Atomic Amazons had never come into our gym. I wished that our first meet was months, not weeks, away. I wished that Darlene had never decided to have her stupid party.

Most of all I wished that Monday would never come. The day that I had to try the Eagle by myself.

None of my wishes came true.

9

Waiting for Fear to Go Away

On Monday, I woke up early. Fear has its up side. I've got to admit that. I felt alert and alive. I was like a thousand-watt stereo system going full blast. It was the day I had made the deal with Patrick to try the Eagle without a spot. I woke up convinced that I could do it.

That feeling lasted until I got out of bed. As I was brushing my teeth, I was sure that I'd never do it without crashing.

I dreaded admitting to Patrick that I was afraid. It was such a wimpy thing to be. I didn't want wimpy to be my style. As soon as we got to the gym I screwed up my courage and asked Patrick if I could talk to him privately.

"Sure," said Patrick. He took me into his office,

a tiny room with barely enough space for a metal desk and two chairs. He sat behind his desk, and waved at a chair. I sat on the edge of it. Patrick leaned forward. "Okay, Cindi, what is it?"

I took a deep breath. "It's my routine on the unevens. I really can't do the Eagle. If we don't change it, I'll foul it up in the meet, and we won't stand a chance. So, for the good of the team, I won't do it."

Patrick leaned back in his chair. " 'The good of the team,' " he repeated. He didn't sound sarcastic, but I wasn't sure. "What exactly scares you?" he asked.

"Huh?" I said, sounding stupid. "I didn't say I was afraid. I just said I couldn't do it, and I think for the good of the team that I shouldn't — "

Patrick waved his hand, cutting me off.

"Think about my question," he said quietly. "Do you remember what I asked?"

"You said I was scared."

Patrick shook his head. "I asked what part of the move scared you. That's different. I'm asking you to think."

"But I didn't say I was scared," I protested. I still didn't want to admit to Patrick that I was terrified to let go of my hands without him spotting me.

Patrick sighed. "Okay, let's back up a little bit."

I nodded. I didn't want to talk about being afraid.

"What conditioning have you been working on the past month?" Patrick asked.

I leaned back in my chair and groaned. "Stomach crunches. . . ."

"Right, Cindi. You're flexible, and you've got quite a bit of upper body strength, but your abdominal muscles were a little weak. So that's what we've been working on since the beginning. And now you're strong."

"Stronger," I admitted. "At least I guess so."

"Now, when you do the Eagle, what do you depend on when you let go of the bar?"

"Nothing," I said. I bit my fingernail. Patrick was coming dangerously close to the moment that I was really afraid of.

"Nothing? You've got nothing to depend on? What holds you there?"

"Nothing," I said quietly. "I can't use my hands."

Patrick shook his head. "Your stomach muscles are what whip you around the bar, and they're stronger now than they ever were. That's why I know you can do it. I've been talking a lot about style lately. But it's not as if you didn't have any. What I've always liked about you is how honest you are. It's not your style to beat around the bush."

"But I . . . I. . . ." I couldn't even hear the nice

things Patrick was saying about me. All I could think of was that I was afraid to do the Eagle on my own.

"Level with me, Cindi. You didn't come in here to discuss 'the good of the team.' Today's Monday. We had a deal that you would do the move without a spot."

"I'm scared," I whispered. "That move really scares me."

"I know it does. Now you're being honest. What part scares you?"

"When I have to let go of my hands, and I'm just hanging there."

"With your stomach muscles controlling your move," said Patrick.

I nodded.

Patrick stood up. "Let's go try it."

I shook my head. "I can't keep my part of the deal. See, now that you know I'm afraid, I don't have to do it, do I?"

Patrick paused. "I'm not going to make you. But I've told you I think you're strong enough to do it. It's got to be your decision. If you don't want to do it, tell me, but don't talk to me about the good of the team."

I hesitated outside Patrick's door. "You mean it?"

For the first time Patrick sounded impatient. "Of course I mean it. But I'm telling you, if you don't try that move now, we're going to forget it, at least for several months. I don't want to waste any more time on it."

"On it or me?" I asked.

"Cindi," said Patrick. "You know that I won't give up on you. Don't ever think that. You can say you won't do the Eagle, and it'll be all right. It's time for you to grow up. You can tell me that you won't do it. I'll respect that."

I sighed. Patrick didn't hate me. He wouldn't even really think of me as a quitter if I didn't make the move. It was up to me.

"Can't we just wait for the fear to go away?" I said.

"It doesn't work that way, Cindi," said Patrick. "I made Monday a deadline, and you agreed. Either we try it now, or we don't."

"Let's try it," I said with a sigh.

"Your decision?" Patrick asked me. "It won't do any good if you're doing it just for me."

"My decision," I said.

Patrick clapped me on the back. "Good," he said. "Let's go out there and do it."

I immediately began to second-guess myself. Maybe it was a lousy decision.

We went out into the gym. The other girls were already warming up. "Go warm up," said Patrick. "I'll take Lauren, Jodi, and Darlene, first. You come when you're ready."

I went over to the mats by the side. Becky was sitting on a bench, her crutches by her side. Patrick had encouraged her to come to the gym whenever she felt like it. She had been showing up to watch us work out almost every day since the accident.

First I did my stretches, ending in a split. Then I lay down to do my sit-ups. I needed someone to hold my legs. I looked around to see if there was anybody else I could ask. Everyone else was working.

"Can you hold my feet?" I asked Becky.

She rolled her eyes as if asking the invalid to move was in the worst taste. She sat down on the mat and held my ankles.

As I did my sit-ups, I could actually feel that they were easier than ever before.

"Are you going to do the Eagle in the meet?" Becky asked.

I grunted yes.

"I don't think you should," said Becky. "You should take it out of your routine. You haven't done it without Patrick spotting you. Besides, it was the move I hurt myself on."

"I'm gonna do it without a spot today," I wheezed. "I've made a deal with Patrick."

"Well, if you foul it up in the meet, you'll ruin it for everybody," I said.

I rolled my eyes. I finished my last sit-up.

"Thanks, Becky," I said. "I know I can always count on you." I stood up.

Becky stared at me. "Well, I was just telling you for your own good," she said. "I'm being honest."

"Yeah, honesty's your style. It's mine, too. Patrick told me so." I held out my hand to help Becky stand up. She grabbed her crutches and hopped across the floor to the uneven bars. I guess she didn't want to miss a disaster.

Patrick was working with Lauren on her floor routine. I chalked up and started swinging from the uneven bars, just to get the feel of it.

Finally Patrick was ready for me. He came and stood to the side of the uneven bars.

"I'll be here if you need me," he said. "Even in the meet, I'll be standing here. But I won't be underneath. When you 'pop,' use your stomach muscles."

I licked my lips. Lauren, Darlene, and Jodi came over to the mats to watch me.

"Good luck," said Lauren.

"We'll buy you a 'pop' if you make it," said Darlene.

Becky said nothing.

I grasped the bar, and started my routine. I swung out from the high bar. I felt my hips hit the low bar. I let go of the high bar and let the momentum carry me around, keeping my stomach as tight as I could.

"POP!" yelled Patrick. I drove my hips against the bar to make use of its bounce. My arms flew out. I reached behind me for the high bar. It was there. I grabbed it. Then I swung out for my dismount and fell on my fanny. I was grinning from ear to ear. I had done it.

I looked up at Patrick. He was grinning, too. "Now, do it again," he said.

"You've got to be kidding," I said.

Patrick shook his head. He held his hand out to me. "You've done it once. Let's see you do it again." Then he paused. "And this time, Cindi, do it with style."

I stuck my tongue out at him. "That's not the kind of style I mean," he said. But he laughed. At least I could still make him laugh.

Trying Isn't Enough

At the end of practice, Patrick called the team over. "What about me?" Becky said.

"You're a part of this team," said Patrick. "Anyone injured is still part of the team. Becky, I want you at the meet, and I want you dressed in an Evergreen uniform."

Our Evergreen uniforms are white with a green pine tree on the chest. I like them a lot. I wished that I could wear mine to Darlene's party. Unfortunately we're not supposed to wear them *except* for team events. I don't think Patrick would consider Darlene's party a team event.

"I'll be glad to wear my Evergreen leotard," said Becky. "With my cast I'll get a lot of attention."

"You'd better tell anyone who asks that Cindi

drew the picture on your cast," said Jodi.

"I will," said Becky, but Jodi winked at me. We both knew that if Becky could take credit for that drawing she would.

"Becky, you take a chair," said Patrick. "The rest of you sit down on the mats. I want to talk to you."

"Why are those words always scary?" asked Lauren.

"This isn't scary, but I want to talk to you again about attitude and style," he said.

I rolled over on the mat and put my hands over my ears. "No, no . . . not more attitude and style. I can't bear it. Let me just live through the meet without style, *puhleeze*?"

"Are you done?" Patrick asked.

I nodded. "Sorry. I just had to get that out of my system."

"This is for all of you," said Patrick. "I want you to think about our attitude from the moment we arrive at the meet. You can't wait to get an attitude once the events begin. Now, most of you have never been to Amazon's Gym. It's fancier than ours. I don't want you walking in there with your mouths hanging open in shock. Walk in as if you own that gym. Appear superconfident even if you have to fake it."

Darlene giggled. But Patrick didn't sound as if he was kidding.

"I mean it," said Patrick. "Meets can be won and lost in the first five minutes. The Amazons will be there to psych you out. I want you prepared. We can do a little psyching out ourselves."

" 'Way to go, Patrick," said Gloria. "But let's be realistic. I mean, we can't win this meet, not without Becky."

Patrick frowned at her. "We've got a great team," he said. "You all have improved incredibly. I don't want you thinking about what might have been. We go with what we've got. Now let me continue."

Patrick flexed his fingers. "I want you to go in there and do the best warm-ups you've ever done in your life. I want you to warm up with a vengeance. Cindi, you're the most flexible. As soon as you're warmed up, go into your split. Don't look around to see who's watching you. The Amazons will be watching. Darlene, when you take your practice on the bars, no hooting."

Darlene hooted. "That was just my last hoot," she said. She giggled.

"Fine," said Patrick. "Remember, you're not just trying to impress the Amazons during the warm-ups. The judges will be watching, too. They'll see whether you mean business or are just a bunch of goof-offs. Now, another thing. Before each event you must salute the judge. Be ready before the judge is. Judges hate it when they have to catch the gymnast's eye because the gymnast is giggling with her friends. When you get the nod from the judge, salute him or her with your hand raised high. Don't make it a wimpy little wave. Afterward, no matter if you screwed up, don't forget to smile at the judge again, and salute. The judge will be impressed that you didn't fall apart from one mistake. Okay, are there any other questions?"

Becky raised her hand. "It's a suggestion," she said. "I think you should give them lessons on how to be good losers."

"We'll be *great* losers," I said. "Winning isn't everything, right, Patrick?"

"I have a lot of faith in all of you," said Patrick. "I'm not worried about your sportsmanship."

Patrick dismissed us. I started for the dressing room, but he called to me, "Enough jokes, Cindi," he said in a low voice. "I didn't appreciate that crack about 'winning isn't everything'."

I stared at him. "I wasn't joking. You said that you liked it that I was honest."

Patrick shook his head. "You think now that you've done the Eagle in practice, no one should expect anything more of you, don't you?"

I blushed. "Well, you said you were proud of me."

"I am, but I won't be if you go into that meet with the attitude that we're bound to lose."

"But, I thought you were the coach who thinks winning isn't everything," I argued.

"I never said that," said Patrick. "Winning may not be everything, but striving and struggling to win is. I've been telling you it's time for you to grow up, Cindi. You can't count on always being the baby, the little girl who scores points just for trying. That's what I meant about finding your own style. I want you to have a style that doesn't say 'baby.'"

I felt as if I were transparent. "I'm not like that," I lied. "I'm sick to death of all this talk about style. What about *losing* with style? Becky was the one who said we should learn to be good losers."

"Becky's angry because she can't compete," said Patrick. "I admire that in her."

Patrick put his arm around me. "I just want you to try your hardest, with no excuses," he said. "You're going to have to trust your own instincts to know whether you've won or not. Just trying isn't enough."

"You're being awfully hard on me," I said. "Why aren't you pushing the others?"

"I am," said Patrick. "And you're ready to be pushed."

"I don't get it," I said. "When is it ever enough? I mean, when will I know if I've tried my hardest? If you won't know, how will I know?"

"You'll know," said Patrick. But I wasn't really sure I would.

11

Outclassed

The morning of the meet, my whole body was tingling. My stomach felt like there was another gymnast living in it, practicing my routines. The feeling in my stomach was a little bit of fear, but it was almost pleasant. It made me feel so alive.

I tried on my Evergreen uniform, white with the green tree on my chest, and I looked at myself in the mirror.

Mom knocked on my door. "You look wonderful," she said. I grimaced.

"I know you're going to be great," she said.

"You can't know that," I said.

Mom smiled at me. "You're wrong. Something's changed in you lately. You're growing up."

"Patrick said I needed to," I said. I took off my uniform, folded it carefully and tucked it into my gym bag. I didn't want it to get wrinkled. Then I put on my warm-up suit.

"He might have been right," said Mom.

My whole family was downstairs at the breakfast table. A package wrapped in tissue paper was sitting on my plate.

"What's that?" I asked.

"It's a present," said Jared. "Isn't that what it looks like?"

"For what? It's not my birthday."

"It's for good luck today," said Dad. "Open it."

I tore open the paper. It was a T-shirt that had my drawing of the girl doing the Eagle silk-screened on it.

Jared smiled at me. "It was my idea. It's the move you're doing today, right? I figured it shouldn't just be on a get-well card. I took it from the computer drawing you made for Becky. It's okay, isn't it? I mean it's *your* drawing."

"It's terrific," I said.

"Are you going to wear it to the meet?" Dad asked.

I shook my head. I didn't want to jinx myself. "I'll wear it afterward," I said. "If I make the move, then I'll have earned it."

"You deserve credit just for trying," said Dad.

I stared at him. "What's wrong?" he asked.

"I don't want that kind of credit," I snapped. My brothers stared at each other.

"Dad didn't mean anything wrong by it," Tim said.

I knew he didn't. "Forget it," I said. "But would you feel good about a football game if your coach said it was good of you just to show up?"

"Of course not," said Tim.

"Then don't give me that kind of credit."

Jared was gawking at me. "What are you staring at?" I demanded.

For a moment I thought I saw respect written on his face. "Nothing," said Jared. "Good luck. I hope you get to wear my T-shirt."

I couldn't eat breakfast. The feeling in the pit of my stomach wouldn't go away.

Jodi's mother picked us up. All the girls competing had to be at the gym two hours before the meet. Jodi was chewing her fingernails.

Lauren had brought Terrance, her teddy bear, along. She introduced Terrance to Jodi and Darlene. I've known Terrance for years. Lauren's had him since she was a baby.

"Isn't he cute?" she said. "I thought maybe he'd bring us luck." She bounced him on the backseat. Only Darlene was quiet.

"Who's nervous?" Jodi's mom asked.

"I'm not," said Darlene. "I thought I would be. But I'm not."

"It's okay to be nervous," said Jodi's mom. "It shows you're alive."

"I'm feeling very alive, then," said Lauren.

"Me, too," I admitted.

We pulled up in front of the Amazon's Gymnastic Center. It was located around the corner from one of the big hotels, and it doubled as a fancy fitness center. The entrance was marble. It looked more like a bank than a gym.

Patrick was standing just inside the lobby, having an intense conversation with Coach Miller. Jodi's mom went up to them. Patrick whispered something in her ear. He looked annoyed. Then he went back to talking to Coach Miller.

Jodi's mom showed us to the dressing room. We were given our own group of lockers. "Where's the competition?" I whispered. The locker room was huge and empty. It had wall-to-wall rose-colored carpeting, and rose-colored lights.

"Hey, check out these mirrors," said Darlene. "They make you look anorexic."

"I'd like to check out the Amazons. Where do you think they are?" I asked.

"Maybe they've forfeited," said Jodi.

Just then the door opened, and Becky hobbled through on her crutches. She was wearing the Evergreen uniform. "There you are," she said. "You're late."

"What are you talking about?" I asked. "We're right on time. The warm-ups are at eleven. The meet isn't until noon."

"Yeah, but the other team's been here since ten. Patrick's really angry. He says Coach Miller told him they couldn't have the gym until eleven because of some aerobics class, and now his team has been here the whole time."

"Great," I said. "Out-psyched before we even start."

"Come on," said Lauren. "Let's go."

"Wait a minute," said Jodi. "I've got to go to the john again."

"Me, too," I said.

"Me three," said Lauren.

We rushed into the bathroom and out again in record time. Darlene started out the door. I followed her with Jodi and Lauren right behind me.

"That's the wrong way," said Becky dryly.

Lauren turned around, bumping into me. I bumped into Jodi, who banged into Darlene.

Becky put her head in her hands. "Great. You look like a bunch of idiots."

"Well, how do you get to the gym?" I asked.

"Follow me," said Becky.

We made our grand, impressive arrival following Becky on crutches. That must have put the fear of God into the other team. The first thing

I noticed were the trophies and medals. They were lined up next to the loudspeakers at the announcer's table, and it looked like there were dozens of them. Surely we could win one of them.

At the last minute I remembered Patrick's advice not to look too impressed. It was hard. There were about twenty girls warming up in the gym. They were all dressed in black leotards with a red zigzag pattern on their chests. Half of them looked twice the age of any of us. I thought we were only supposed to be working out against their Class III and IV girls.

One girl whizzed past me and did a handspring with a 360° turn on the vault, a move that I couldn't do in a million years.

Patrick came up to us and herded us over to a corner of the mats. He smiled, but he looked tense. "Okay," he said. "I want you to begin your warm-ups."

"How many Amazons are there?" I asked.

"We'll just be competing against their intermediate girls. But Coach Miller is letting his whole team warm up. Don't let them intimidate you."

I swallowed hard as one of the Amazons did a routine on the uneven bars that was spectacular. The audience applauded. And that was just her warm-up.

"Cindi," commanded Patrick. "Start stretching now. I want to see your splits."

I sighed. I was pretty sure that my splits were not going to impress this crowd.

"We're sunk," said Lauren. "Becky was right. We don't have a prayer."

"Think bubble," said Darlene, as she stretched out. "We're in a bubble of concentration."

"We're in a bubble of hot soup," I said. "We're in trouble."

I heard the crowd applaud someone else. I knew right away we were outclassed, and I wasn't just psyching myself out. I was being honest. After all Patrick had said honesty was my style. And honestly, these girls were *way* better than we were.

What If Your Best Isn't Good Enough?

Our warm-ups were a disaster. The spring-board for the vault felt totally different from the one at our gym. Everytime I tried a vault, I crashed. Even the floor mats were much bouncier than ours. My whole rhythm on my floor routine felt off. And I was doing okay compared to my teammates. Jodi tripped doing a simple one-handed cartwheel on her floor routine. She landed hard.

"I'm okay," she said. She tried it again, and fell over backward.

We could hear the Amazons tittering about us in the background as we practiced our routines. Suddenly I noticed two women and a man come into the gym. They didn't sit in the spectator area. They came right out to the middle of the gym, and both Patrick and Coach Miller jumped to greet them. They were all three wearing identical blazers.

"The judges," whispered Darlene.

"How do you know?" I asked.

"I can tell by the uniforms. The USGF judges always wear those blazers."

I immediately went into my best split. I could feel my hamstrings pulling. "Look serious," I warned Jodi, who was trying a handstand pirouette, a move she really can't do. She fell. I heard a gasp from the crowd. Jodi's fall hadn't been that bad. I looked around to see what Amazon had just completed another dazzling trick.

For the moment the spectators were not paying any attention to us gymnasts. Darlene's mom and dad had come in and were sitting in the back, next to my parents and brothers. They tried to look inconspicuous, but it's hard to hide someone who's six feet four and weighs two hundred and forty pounds.

About a dozen kids ran up to Big Beef for autographs. Darlene looked embarrassed. "Don't worry," I whispered. "They won't know he's your dad."

"Cindi, I'm the only black girl on our team. Whose dad do you think they'll think he is?"

"Maybe they'll think he adopted my brothers,"

I said. "They're hanging around him like bodyguards."

Darlene looked up. "I should be used to it," she said.

"Come on," I said. "This is *our* day to shine, not his."

"Shine? We're gonna be buried by the Amazons," said Lauren. "Do you see anybody who isn't better than us?" Lauren asked.

I looked around. I had to admit the answer was no.

Patrick came over to us. "Our first official event will be the vault," he said. He looked at our faces. "What's wrong?"

"We're outclassed even before we begin," said Jodi.

Patrick cut her off. He looked angry. "Don't ever say that," he said. "You are good and you've worked hard. You're every bit as good as these girls. I wouldn't trade any of you. Now just go out there and have fun."

"Have fun?" exclaimed Jodi.

"That's right," said Patrick. "And remember. There's nothing more fun than winning."

The announcer spoke into a microphone. "Good afternoon, ladies and gentlemen. Welcome to the Atomic Amazons' Challenge. Later this afternoon, we will have a contest of our elite competitors, but first we have a special treat for you.

96

Patrick Harmon's Evergreen Team has agreed to compete against the Amazons' intermediate team. Girls, you can begin your one touch warm-up."

"One touch warm-up" means that each of us gets a final chance to practice on the apparatus. If you fall off once you lose your turn.

I chalked up for the Eagle. I did my mount, and I was doing fine. Patrick stood to the side. "Now," he said. I cast out from the high bar, trying to keep my arms straight. When I felt my hips hit the low bar, I shouted "pop" to myself. I didn't fall. But I didn't have the momentum to get around. I slipped off the bar. I was one eagle who crash-landed. I had lost my turn to practice.

One of the Atomic Amazons, a short girl with her hair in two bunches by her ears, started to chalk up. "I hate the Eagle," she said.

I agreed. I moved off the mat beneath the bars to give her room.

Patrick squatted beside me. "You were doing fine, but you lost it," he said. "If that happens during the competition, just go into another hip circle, using your hands. You don't have to complete the Eagle if it isn't going right. It's your judgment call. Don't go for it if it doesn't feel right."

"*Now* you tell me," I said.

"I want you to go for it," said Patrick. "But no

one but you is going to know how you feel up there. If you don't think you have it, go for the easier routine."

I nodded.

"Two-minute warning, girls," said the announcer.

I swallowed hard. I watched the girl from the Amazon team practice her routine. I could have killed her. *She* did the Eagle beautifully. And did she have style! The way she held her hands as she reached back, the confidence with which she swung just made you want to watch her. I studied her.

The Eagle looked magnificent when it was done right. But I knew she had tried to psych me out when she told me she hated it.

"I fell off the beam after six seconds," said Lauren, coming up to me and giggling.

"Look at that girl," I said, pointing to the girl in pigtails. "She's really good. And she tried to psych me out."

Darlene came and plopped down next to us. "I am *so* nervous," she said. "I wasn't nervous before. Why do I have to get nervous now? I just went to the bathroom and already I feel like I have to pee again."

I patted her on the back. We watched Jodi practicing her floor routine. She got all the tumbling moves, but Jodi really wasn't a good dancer. She moved awkwardly between moves. She finished and came to sit with us.

"We don't have a prayer," said Jodi, breathing hard.

Darlene waved to her father, who was taking pictures.

"Hey," I said. "Cut it out."

"Cut what out?" asked Darlene. "I was just waving at my folks."

"Not you. I meant Jodi. Saying we don't have a prayer. I've been saying stuff like that, too. We gotta stop talking like that. Who's our coach?"

Jodi, Lauren, and Darlene looked at me as if I had gone batty.

"Who's our coach?" I repeated.

Jodi looked at Darlene and Lauren. "Has she lost her mind?"

"Who's our coach?" I insisted.

"Patrick Harmon," said Jodi finally. She giggled.

"Is he or is he not a thousand times nicer and better than their creep?"

Darlene nodded.

"Would Patrick send us out to be eaten by lions?" I asked.

"Amazons," said Lauren. "But remember, we were the ones who talked Patrick into letting us come here."

"In fact, *you* were the one who talked him into it," said Darlene.

"Well, let's show him what we're made of," I said. I held my palm into the middle of our group the way I had seen my brothers do.

Jodi slapped it first, then Darlene, then Lauren. "Aw-right!" I shouted. "TIM*BER* . . . !"

Patrick came over to us and squatted down on his heels. "Is that the team cheer?" he asked.

"We're going to win this one for you," I said.

Patrick shook his head. "Win this one for yourselves," he said. "Just do your best."

The announcer tapped the microphone. "Ladies and gentlemen, we are about to begin. Our first event will be the vault. First up will be Lauren Baca. Darlene Broderick on deck. Cindi Jockett is in the hole." A cheer went up that seemed to fill the gymnasium. It was my brothers.

We stood up and hugged each other. We walked over as a team to the runway for the vault. Becky was leaning against the wall. The officials had allowed her onto the meet floor because Patrick had told them she was officially part of the team.

"What did Patrick tell you?" Becky asked.

"He told us to do our best," I said as Lauren got ready for her first vault.

"Your best isn't gonna be good enough here," said Becky. "These girls are really good."

"Thanks, Becky," I said. "With you as a cheer-leader we can't lose."

"I'm just being honest," said Becky.

"Shut up," I said. I shook out my arms and legs, like a swimmer about to dive into the deep end. I was scared.

13

A Technical Knockout

On her first vault, Lauren forgot to salute the judge. The judge was sitting on a folding chair at the far end of the runway by the horse.

"Lauren Baca," he called out. He sounded annoyed. Lauren turned bright red. She held up her hand to salute him. Then she began her run. She was running hard, but she hit the board with the wrong foot, and she couldn't get her jump. She just kept going and half-fell into the vault, trying to brake with her hands. She didn't attempt to get over it.

Even when you completely foul up a vault you're supposed to turn and salute the judge. Lauren forgot until Patrick hissed at her. She turned and half-raised her right hand.

She came back to us practically in tears. "Don't worry," I said. "You've got another chance." Unfortunately Lauren missed her next vault, too. She was disqualified on the vault, and it was her best event.

None of us did much better on the vault, and we did even worse on our floor routines. At the end of those two events the score was Atomic Amazons 66.5, Evergreens 26.3. We were being slaughtered.

"Too bad gymnastics isn't like boxing," said Becky. "The judges would call this off out of mercy."

Patrick frowned at her. "We have our two best events still to go," he said.

"Right," said Becky, sarcastically.

"Right," I echoed. I was one of the ones who had scored lowest on my floor routine. "Let's show them what we're made of."

"Give me Terrance Teddy," said Lauren. "I forgot to kiss him for good luck." Lauren gave Terrance a kiss on his furry nose.

"What good will that do?" said Becky. She really was a pain. I wished Patrick hadn't let her on the floor.

"Wait and see," said Lauren.

I don't know if it was kissing Teddy or what,

but Lauren redeemed herself on the beam. She went through her routine without a mistake, but it wasn't a very risky routine and the judges only scored her 6.1. I thought it was unfair, and I told Patrick so.

"They just want to leave room for the rest of you. Don't sweat it," he said.

He gave Lauren a hug. I kissed her and handed back Teddy. "Give him to me," said Jodi. "If he worked for you, maybe he'll work for me."

She gave Terrance a big smack.

Terrance's luck was nontransferable. Jodi was awful. She missed her mount and fell from the beam, and she never seemed to get her balance again. She fell off a second time in her first cat leap, the one she did so beautifully in practice. I could see how frustrated she was getting. She didn't take time to gather herself. She was allowed thirty seconds to remount, and Patrick had told us to take the time. Jodi scrambled back on the beam right away, and she fell off in her next move, her forward roll. When she finally finished her routine she had only scored 4.5.

Then it was Darlene's turn, and she was wonderful. I had never seen her look so graceful and concentrated. She went full out on her moves, and she did her roundoff dismount better than

I had ever seen it. She saluted the judges with a big smile on her face.

I jumped up to give her a hug when she finished. "Way to go," I said.

"Now we're showing them what we're made of."

Darlene grinned. But she only scored a 6.6. "It's up to you," she said.

I tried to remember Patrick's bubble of concentration. I saluted the judges and smiled at them. Then I let my face get serious as I tried to picture my mount.

I jumped on the beam into my split. It was a move I had done a thousand times perfectly. But somehow my knees rolled in, and I just kept rolling and fell off the beam, landing hard on my shoulder.

Patrick moved toward me. I shook him off. I stood up. I knew I had thirty seconds to remount. I put my hands on the beam and pushed up. I remounted. But when I did my forward somersault, my hips got off-angle and I had to grasp the bottom of the beam to keep from rolling off, another automatic .3 deduction.

It was so strange. I didn't feel awful. My legs weren't shaking or anything. Normally the beam is the only event for which I really do feel that I have a style. But my style wasn't helping me today. I just couldn't do anything right. I fell again just doing a little leap. By the time my routine was finished, I knew I had ruined any chance our team had to win the beam. My score was 5.1.

The very first Atomic Amazon up scored a 6.8, and their scores only got higher.

Maybe Becky was right. Maybe the judges should have called it a technical knockout.

14

It's Not Over
Till It's Over

"Last licks," said Patrick, as they announced that the Atomic Amazons and the Evergreen team would perform on the uneven bars. "Are you ready?"

"Last licks; they should call it last rites," said Becky.

"That's enough," said Patrick. "Becky, go sit with the spectators."

"What?" exclaimed Becky.

"You heard me," said Patrick. "These girls are trying their hearts out and all you've done all day is put them down. I'm sick of it. Go sit with the spectators until you can feel part of this team."

Becky glared at him. "If I hadn't hurt myself we wouldn't be such a laughing stock," she said.

"Go sit down," said Patrick. Becky grabbed her crutches and hobbled to the side.

"All right," said Patrick. "This is your last chance. But you haven't done that badly. None of you gave up. You've showed a lot of style." Patrick winked at me when he said the word "style."

"I don't get it," I said angrily. "You're just saying that. I've done nothing but foul up. How can you say I did it with style? That sounds like something you'd say to a little kid to make her feel better. I don't need that kind of pap."

The others looked shocked that I would talk back to Patrick. Only Patrick didn't look surprised. "I'm not patronizing you," he said. "Cindi, you showed style when you didn't give up on the beam even though you didn't have *it* today. That happens in gymnastics. Before, I always felt you held something back, just in case you failed. When I talked about 'style' I didn't want a completely *new* Cindi. I just wanted a Cindi who was all the way out there."

"Out there," I repeated. "Yeah, I was so far out that I was off the beam."

Patrick nodded. "That was true today, but it won't be the next time. Now you know what it feels like to go full out. It's different from being far out," he said.

"And what about my style?" I asked. I was still a little angry.

"Cindi, I just wanted more from you. Go full out. That's the style I want from you."

"That seems too simple," I said.

Patrick smiled at me. "Sometimes a simple style is the best."

The Atomic Amazons went ahead of us on the unevens. Finally we would have a chance to see what they would do before us. The first Amazon got stuck trying to get to the high bar. She had to jump off, regroup, and put her feet on the low bar to get up to the high bar. Her dismount was shaky, too.

Our team grinned at each other. I know you're not supposed to show emotion if the other team fouls up, but the Atomic Amazons had shown plenty of emotion when we had screwed up.

The next two Amazons didn't do too well, either. Then it came time for the girl in the pigtails. The one who had tried to out-psych me. She saluted the judge with a beaming smile. She reminded me of somebody who wanted to be the teacher's pet.

She did her mount as if there was no way she could miss, and she had a lot of strength — I'll give her that. She did the first part of the Eagle beautifully. She whipped around the lower bar

with no hands. Maybe it was overconfidence, because when she arched up and threw her hands
wide, she missed the high bar, just like Becky
did. She would have fallen completely if her
coach, Darrell Miller, hadn't leaped up to steady
her.

Then, on her dismount, she fell on her knees
after landing, an automatic .5 fault.

The judges awarded her a 7.4, higher than any
of the other Amazons had scored. I thought it
was too high, considering she hadn't even completed the Eagle, the most difficult element in her
routine.

Then it was our turn. Last licks indeed. Jodi
was fantastic on the uneven bars. She found a
rhythm early in her routine, and instead of her
usual foul-ups, she completed it beautifully, even
sticking her dismount. The judges awarded her
a 6.2, which I thought was low considering how
good she was. I wished that Patrick hadn't put
her first.

But then Darlene and Lauren also got through
their routines beautifully, too. Lauren got a 6.6,
and Darlene a 6.8.

It was my turn. Lauren held Terrance out for
me. I kissed the top of his head. Then I went to
the bin to chalk up.

Patrick clapped his arm on my shoulder. "If

you get a 8.1 we can win this event," he whispered.

I nodded. "No pressure, huh?"

He grinned at me. "I just thought you'd want to know."

"Hey, don't sweat it," said Lauren. "We've all fouled up once or more."

"Lauren's right," said Jodi. "There's no way we can win this meet. Even if we win the uneven bars, it doesn't really count. They've got the meet sewed up."

"Maybe the meet. But we can still win one event. It's not over till it's over, as Yogi Berra says," I said.

"Who's Yogi Berra?" asked Jodi.

"Just my favorite old-time baseball player," I said. "He wasn't a quitter."

"Cynthia Jockett?" asked the judge.

I saluted and smiled. I hoped my smile looked more natural than it felt.

I closed my eyes for a moment and took a deep breath. When I opened my eyes I wasn't smiling. My style wasn't cute. I was a competitor.

I grasped the bar and swung up into my mount. My arms were straight. I could feel myself pulling out to a full extension.

Then it was time to either fly or not. I took a deep breath. "Breathe," I heard Patrick whisper.

I knew he was there. I pulled up, my chest high and began my swing.

"Fly!" I said to myself. That's my style. I'm a flyer. I let go and wrapped my hips around the lower bar.

"POP!" I said to myself as my legs neared the floor. I used all my stomach muscles to reach out like an eagle flying. I reached behind me.

The bar was there. I grabbed it. Then I re-grasped, swung back down to a belly "beat" off the low bar. I was grinning. I couldn't help myself.

I opened my legs and straddled the low bar, letting myself swing backward for my dismount. I actually had too much swing. I landed heavy, and I had to take two full steps after landing. But that was only a .2 fault.

I heard my team screaming out its cheers. Patrick raised his hand. I gave him a high five.

15

Winning Is a Great Style

Lauren jumped up and hugged me. I looked back at the uneven bars. I couldn't believe that I had actually done the Eagle in competition. I had done it! And I had done it with style. There's an old blues song about holding on to a dollar " 'til the eagle grins." I was grinning.

I waited for the judges. The scores went up. 8.2. The highest scores I had ever gotten on any event! We had won!

Patrick came over and gave me a bear hug.

The announcer's voice came over the loud-speaker. "We will have a five-minute break while we tabulate the scores," he said.

"What do they have to tabulate?" asked Jodi.

"Cindi won the unevens. They won everything else."

Becky hobbled over. "Congratulations," she said.

"Thanks," I said. I figured I could afford to be nice. "If you had been there maybe we would have won more than one event."

"You were lucky that girl fouled up her Eagle," said Becky.

I shook my head at her. "You're wrong, Becky. I wasn't lucky. I earned those extra points."

I turned away from her and went back to my friends, my real teammates, Lauren, Darlene, and Jodi.

Finally the announcer declared that the tabulations were complete. They set up a victory platform in the center of the floor. It wobbled.

First he announced the individual winners for the vault. It was a sweep for the Atomic Amazons. We had to sit there while the three Atomic Amazons all hugged and kissed each other. Their coach hung medals with red, white, and blue ribbons around their necks.

Next he announced the winners on the beam. Once again all three winners were from the Atomic Amazons.

It was the same for the floor exercises. The Atomic Amazons were laughing, and even some of the spectators tittered at how often the announcer had to keep repeating the same names.

Then he announced the winners for the uneven bars. Lauren, Jodi, and Darlene hugged me again. Third place was an Atomic Amazon. Second place was Bernodette Sawyer, the girl in the pigtails. It was only her fourth medal. She hardly had room around her neck for any more.

Then they announced the winner. Me. Cindi Jockett. I heard my brothers screaming and stamping their feet. They didn't embarrass me. I felt great.

I walked up to the winners' platform. I held out my hand to Bernodette Sawyer and the other Amazon.

Then I took a big jump onto the winners' step. I was so tall, I loved it.

Coach Miller handed the medal to Patrick. He walked up. I had to lower my head to let Patrick put the medal around my neck. As I did, he whispered into my ear, "Winning is a great style, isn't it?" he said.

"I could get used to it," I whispered back. I waved to my parents and brothers. Then I stepped down.

Darlene gave me a kiss. "I like your style," she said.

I grinned at her.

"I know what I'm wearing to your party," I said.

Darlene raised her eyebrow, and fingered my medal. "And what's that?" she asked.

"Something that I don't have to worry about anyone else wearing," I said. "Not even Becky."

"Now we will award the team trophies," said the announcer. We had to sit down again while the Atomic Amazons picked up their trophies for the beam, the floor exercises, and the vault.

Then he announced the uneven bars. "Patrick Harmon's Evergreens," said the announcer. Even though two Amazons had come in second and third, our team had been more consistent, and with my high score we had won.

The whole place erupted into applause. It might be the Amazon's home gym, and the Amazons would win the all-around, but my brothers and Big Beef could make an awful lot of noise. We jumped up and hugged each other. The announcer handed us our trophy.

"You really earned this," Lauren said to me.

"No, we all did," I said.

Then I looked over to the sidelines and saw Patrick looking proud. "I know who this trophy really belongs to," I said. "Let's give it to him,"

All together, as a team, we carried our trophy to Patrick.

16

We All Got Style

Jared knocked on my door for the sixth time. "Are you ready?" he asked.

I looked at myself in the mirror. The bed behind me was piled with the entire contents of my closet. I think I had tried on absolutely everything I owned.

I have to admit that a medal is one piece of jewelry that looks great on anything. I tried it on with turtlenecks and jeans. I tried it on with my velvet dress for Christmas. It looked good with them all. Finally I decided on my jeans, cowboy boots, and purple turtleneck. I liked the purple against the red, white, and blue ribbon of my medal.

I took one look at myself in the mirror again.

My medal had a gymnast doing a split embossed on one side. It was as if it were made for me.

I ran my finger over the engraving. I took the medal off, and looked at myself in the mirror without it. I *was* the only one to win a medal. Would it be bragging to wear it?

Sure it would. But what was wrong with bragging? I had won it. Like I told Becky, I had earned it.

"Cindi," shouted Jared. "We'll be late."

"You're only invited to this party because she's my friend," I said. "I'm not ready." I put the medal back around my neck and took one final look at myself in the mirror. I definitely looked better with it on.

Then I looked again. I remembered Darlene, Jodi, and Lauren hugging me when I finished my routine. I thought about Darlene on the beam. She had been incredible, and she hadn't won a medal, not even third place.

And Lauren screwing up so terribly on the vault, our first event. I mean, such a total screw-up that she never even got over the vault.

And yet, when it really counted, she had performed on the bars.

Jodi. Jodi was always unpredictable. She was the one who almost always screwed up. But she had worked hard, too, and done a terrific routine on the bars. Together we had won a trophy.

118

Sure, I had something that Becky didn't have. I had my medal. But none of my friends had medals, either. We had gone into that meet as a team. I took the medal off and hung it over the corner of the mirror.

Jared knocked on the door again.

"One minute," I shouted. I had something else that no one else had. My T-shirt. I had designed it. Maybe Jared had the idea of putting the sketch on the shirt for me, but I had drawn it. It showed a girl doing an Eagle, a move I had mastered.

I put on the T-shirt, then I put on the medal over it. The medal looked great against the shirt. I thought about what Patrick had said, "Sometimes a simple style is best." He had wanted more of me, and I had tried harder this afternoon than I had ever tried for anything in my life. When I went for the Eagle, I hadn't held anything back. That was my style. I didn't need the medal to prove it. I put the medal back on the mirror. I'd be able to look at it every day. I would wear a T-shirt and jeans. But it was a very special T-shirt.

"I'm ready," I shouted.

"It's about time," said Jared.

I opened the door.

"You're wearing my T-shirt," he said. He looked proud. "It looks good."

"Thanks," I said simply. Then I giggled. Giggling is my style, too.

Tim drove us over to the Brodericks. They live in a large, modern one-story house made of stone and glass. Darlene's mom opened the door. She gave me a kiss. "Congratulations, Cindi. You were terrific today."

I introduced her to Jared. "We met at the meet," she said. She shook Jared's hand. I was surprised to see Jared blushing.

"The party's in the basement," she said.

Jared and I climbed down the steps. I heard the music and people laughing. I was actually glad Jared was there. I felt shy. I hadn't been to many parties, especially one in a fancy house with mostly older kids, kids in the sixth and seventh grades.

Down in the rec room, Darlene waved to me. She was surrounded by kids I didn't know. She looked great. She was wearing baggy pants, with suspenders, over a purple sweater. It was the kind of outfit only Darlene could pull off.

I looked around and saw Lauren and Jodi sitting on a couch at the side of the room. They looked out of place, too.

I went over to them. They both looked so happy to see me. I realized they felt as shy I did.

Lauren looked great in her new red jumpsuit. Jodi looked terrific. Her hair was in a neat braid with purple and gold ribbons tied into it. She wore Jared's jacket and black baggy pants.

"I like your T-shirt," said Lauren.

"Jared made it for me out of my computer drawing," I said.

"Becky's gonna be jealous," said Jodi. "She thinks she's the only eagle."

"You guys will be learning it soon. When you do, I'll get Jared to make you T-shirts, too. Maybe we can graduate from Pinecones to Eagles."

"Right," said Jodi.

We watched the other kids at the party. It was very weird. Normally the three of us would be talking and laughing a blue streak, but outside of gymnastics class it was like we didn't know what to say. And none of the kids from St. Agnes seemed interested in talking to us.

We watched the party, all of us feeling a little out of it.

I heard someone clumping down the stairs. "Becky," said Lauren with a giggle. Since Becky went to St. Agnes she knew most of the kids. Becky spotted us.

I waved.

Becky hopped over to our couch. "Do you want a seat?" I asked, starting to stand up.

Darlene came and joined us.

"Where's your medal?" Becky asked me.

"It's home," I said.

Darlene stared at me. "I thought you would wear it tonight," she said. "Why didn't you?"

"I was *sure* you'd be wearing it," said Becky. "It's the kind of tacky thing kids usually do with their first medal."

"It's not my style," I said, smiling. I didn't need to tell her how close I had come to wearing it.

Darlene grinned at me. "I like your T-shirt," she said. "Hey, guys," she shouted to her friends. "These kids here are my gymnastics pals. We're on the same team."

Darlene's friends came over. Darlene introduced us all. "We had a meet today and Cindi here won a medal," said Darlene.

Her friends looked impressed.

"We all won a trophy," I said.

"Show us some moves," said one of her friends. I saw Jared leaning against the wall. He winked at me. He turned up the speakers and put on some music with a good backbeat.

"Show them the one that makes me go 'ouch' " said Jared.

I stood up and did a split.

"Let's show 'em our handstands into a forward roll," said Darlene. Her friends cleared a space for us and started clapping in time to the music.

Jodi, Darlene, Lauren, and I did handstands.

"Hey, you guys are really good," said one of Darlene's friends.

I stood up. My face was flushed. We all grabbed hands. "TIM*BER* . . . !" I yelled. We dropped hands and together did back somersaults,

"What a team," somebody said.

"You'd better believe it," I said. Then we all giggled and started to dance. We got the whole party dancing. Gymnasts are great dancers. We got style.

WIN A BRAND NEW GYMNASTICS WARDROBE!

Announcing...

THE GYMNASTS™

CONTEST!

Flip for gymnastics! You're invited to enter The Gymnasts Contest—YOU can win a fantastic gymnastics wardrobe, including a duffel bag, valued at $100.00! It's easy! Just complete the coupon below and return by December 31, 1988.

Watch for *Nobody's Perfect #3*
coming in November wherever you buy books!